This Great Divide

Short Stories

This Great Divide

Eric Prochaska

HALO FORGE PRESS, LLC
2006

Published by
Halo Forge Press, LLC
20 Lowell Avenue
Bisbee, Arizona 85603
www.haloforgepress.com

First paperback edition

ISBN 0-9772349-0-8

"Thunder on a Clear Day" originally appeared in *The Morpo Review*
"Interred With the Bones" originally appeared in *Whistling Shade*
"Cerberus on the Mogollon Rim" and "Reservations" originally appeared in *American Western Magazine*
"This Great Divide" originally appeared in *InterText*
"Nothing but Infinity" originally appeared in *Mobius: The Journal of Social Change*
"Long-Term Maintenance" originally appeared in *Amarillo Bay*
"Exhale" originally appeared in *Seeker*
"My Garden Which Never Grows" originally appeared in *Moondance*
"His Two Hearts" originally appeared in *Dakota House Journal*

To my family and friends.

To the heritage of writers whose stories captivated my imagination.

To Kay Bach
Who believed in me and set me on the path. When you told me you expected to see my name in print someday, I was listening.

To Carl Albert
Who taught me to write and rewrite. I always carry your lessons with me.

To Yoon Jeong
Who always listens. This is what I've been trying to say.

To God
Who is patient, forgiving, loving, and understanding. I only hope to bring you glory.

This Great Divide

Short Stories

by

Eric Prochaska

This Great Divide

Indoor Plumbing for Posterity

From any overlook along the Mogollon Rim the valley of shifting sand and sidewinders below, prickly with its heat and cacti, is nothing more than breakers receding into an ocean contained between the Bradshaw Mountains on the west and the Colorado Plateau to the north. On days when the smog stain which hovers above the Phoenix conglomerate is blown to New Mexico you can inhale with the serenity provided by the fantasy that the metropolis has eroded away.

High country. The Colorado Plateau. Judy Garland's mention of Flagstaff on a train in *The Harvey Girls* is likely all they've heard of this place. So when they drive their kids out I-40 to see the Grand Canyon they are surprised to traverse through an hour of ponderosa pine forest, stretching all the way to Williams, where they head north to see the Big Ditch. If they come across a herd of pronghorn or elk, they veer onto the shoulder, skid to a stop and snap off their whole roll of film. I guess I don't blame 'em. Compared to Atlanta or Tampa, northern Arizona must be as exotic as the African veldt. Mt. Humphries looming in lieu of Mt. Kenya.

But most of those families never stray far enough from the interstate to discover Cliffside. The kids get too rambunctious in the car, and there isn't a big ticket attraction around here to entice their attention, so the folks pack it back up and head on home. I'll tell you what: I don't mind that a bit. This is our home. After toiling under Lewis Kingman for the Santa Fe Railroad, our great great grandfathers settled here, raised sons to move down and mine Jerome, then move back with sons to help with the cattle, whose sons worked the saws and lathes at the molding mill. Despite the trickle of weekenders up from the valley in the summer, plus the more romantic yuppie couples who enjoy the forest, we're no tourist trap. Just a pit stop between ancient ruins, fishing holes, and cabin hideaways. Anyhow, that's how it was when I was a kid. But a lot would change before I grew up.

In the end, I used the money I had saved up from working at Lincoln's gas station to get as far away from Cliffside as possible. Not that I ever stopped loving my hometown. But sometimes it hurts to see what becomes of the things you love, and it's better to just put some distance between you, to save your own heart.

"So, how far is it to the Mogollon rim?" the guy in the hunter green golf shirt asked as his Toyota Landcruiser guzzled premium from the pump and I stood on my tiptoes to make swipes across his windshield from the top down, hoping the woman inside would stretch her arms over her head to pull the spaghetti string top tighter. Hey, I was a teenager, so give me a break. Besides, it was a small town, and you cherished what gifts were sent your way. Still, her boyfriend—or fiancé more likely—was tapping that folded map against his thigh behind me, waiting for a response.

"It's pronounced Mo-gee-yon," I told him.

"What?"

"It's the Mo-gee-yon Rim. You said Mo-go-lon. Looks like it would be pronounced that way, but it's a Native American word and it's pronounced Mo-gee-yon."

"Oh," he said, not angrily. "So, how do we get there?"

" Well, you're on it, pretty much. But I guess you want to look over the edge. So stay on the highway and in about seven miles there's a turnoff. Head left. The trees will thin out in a few miles, and there'll be a tight turn around a guardrail. You don't want to try slowing down for the view right there, all right? You wouldn't believe how many people get rear-ended along that stretch. Just after the guard rail there's a pull off."

"Just stay on this highway, then turn left, right?"

"You got it. You know, if you have a camera, there's no better place around here to take a picture. In fact, if you stayed in town about an hour or so, maybe grabbed a bite over there at Stump's Diner," I said, indicating the diner down the block, "you'd get there just before sunset. You really have to get a picture of an Arizona sunset before you head back to Kansas."

"How'd you know— Oh. The license plates. Well, is the food over there any good?"

"Best in town," I lied. That was my job, as I saw it. Not lying, just directing out-of-towners to spend a little more money in town, as long as they were there. But I wouldn't have sold my soul over it.

My stint as a gas station attendant started during the summer before my junior year and lasted until a few months after graduation. But the events which would force me to abandon Cliffside were already in motion by then.

The pasture land north of town was surrounded by hills of piny-on pines and juniper, with the tall ponderosa pines beyond that. One strike during a breezy summer lightning storm can set a tidal wave of flames flooding across the landscape—and it did. From near a dry creek bed in the far part of the Taylor ranch, the glow oozed over the rise, sneaking toward town. Firefighters and ranch hands stumbled over each others' efforts to stomp out the flames while they were still in the open range. As we were driving by that night, many of us pulled to the side of the road to stop and watch the silhouettes of the men dashing back and forth in front of the stripe of jagged light which didn't seem so threatening from the highway. This may be why the other fire was not noticed until it was too late.

Inside the church, the light through the high arched windows relegated every shadow that might have lingered in the oak roof beams to a hiding place under the pews. My family was a church-going family, which I don't mention to make any claims of superiority over anyone else, but I guess it's important to know that my father and mother appreciated the duty of raising a son in the faith, and that that church was literally the House of God in my young mind. Anyhow, back then, it wasn't really a question of who did or didn't go to church, but who went to which church. There was only one in town, and that sat on the top of a steep knoll clear of trees, but with forest all around. It was nicknamed Baldy Peak, not because it was as large as the one of the same name over by Greer, but because it just resembled a bald man's dome, rising over the thick forest.

During the week, the dirt parking lot at the base of the knoll served as a baseball field for the younger kids, not big enough to ever lay claim to the grass field at the high school when older kids were around. So we'd ride our bikes out there, play our game, and drink the water our mothers made sure we took with us under the shady side of the church. Laying on my back in the grass, looking up at its upside-down mass painted dark by the sun it hid, I had the impression of a huge Gothic castle atop some dreary peak. Not that it had a tall steeple, or was truly enormous, but I suppose just the immense cut stones which lined the foundation and rose up in perfect-posture stacks to support the roof at the corners lent it such a deceiving weight. Those stones were not the red rocks of Arizona fame, but tons of gray stone carted down by a dozen of our great grandfathers from somewhere in the Rockies after they had quit the railroad to settle here. The trip took two months, our Sunday school teacher would tell us, and one man died when a cart of stone they were easing down a pass thickly littered with treacherous shards of stones proved too much for the ropes and snatched that man who was guiding the load—Elijah Simms—along as it hurtled itself into the ravine below. His own brother, Isaiah Simms, whose son would found the long-standing Stump's Diner decades later, watched in horror along with the ten other men, who then would have to descend into the canyon to retrieve the blocks of stone and gather up the bloody, limp body to carry until they reached a valley with soil suitable for a burial. How could anyone not understand the resolve of our ancestors? Such travail was not undertaken for themselves. They were establishing a cornerstone for centuries of generations to build upon.

It must have been lightning, though no one saw it, that ignited the second fire while we sat on the hoods of cars and tailgates of trucks, lobbing whimsical remarks about the hustling men up and down the line of spectators.

"Hey! You missed a spot!" someone two cars down called when the fire was nearly out. Of course the firemen were out of earshot. It was like talking back to a movie screen, meant to impress the other viewers with your wit.

About that time, while the ranch hands were loading into trucks and heading in toward the Taylor place, a solitary car came tearing at us from town. It was Mrs. Prescott, who worked in the post office. She slowed down as if to get a view of the fire which was all but dead now, but then she stopped in the middle of the highway, emerged from her car and shouted over the roof to all of us who were lingering as if watching all the credits roll at the end of the feature, "The church is on fire!"

"What? What's that?" they called to have the news relayed down the line.

One by one, three dozen heads turned in the same direction across the rolling mounds of treetops to find the undulating afterglow of those pioneer dreams two miles and far too late away. Commands were shouted for someone to get the fire department as the caravan of engines were ignited like rolling thunder.

This suddenly humorless congregation arrived at the church, left our car doors gaping open as we sleepwalked to the foot of the rise, atop which the flames were several feet high. Humbled, I was, amid the throng of hands dangling open along the still legs which led to the necks which were tilted both back and somehow away from the crown of flames.

Exclamations in the tone of "Oh, Dear Lord!" were whispered apologetically, but those are not prayers we expect to be answered.

Before the fire truck could replenish the tank of water it had expelled on the Taylor range, the timber roof of the church had tumbled inward. Like a whale purging its blow hole, the church coughed a swirling galaxy of fireflies into the featureless sky, where they relaxed and drifted over our heads, cooled to ash and descended into our eyes, bringing tears.

Furious, I grew. Not that the church burnt down. No. That could not have been foreseen. But when the stone walls still stood as constant as ever, how could they talk of abandoning the church to build a completely new one?

"All they have to do is put a new roof on it," I said. My father had the case from the chain saw engine removed already, and was wiping away the build-up of sawdust and grease from the border like a tan-line where it had come off.

"Are you paying attention? I expect you to be able to do this yourself next time."

"I'm watching," I said, though I wasn't. My eyes were facing his hands, turning over the core of the saw on the workbench, but they refused to focus. "I just don't see why they want to build a new church."

"Well, like they said, the old church doesn't even have proper electricity, and no plumbing and no phone lines."

"Who needs a phone at church, anyway?"

"I don't know about that, but there have been a few times when a bathroom would have saved me some anguish."

"Very funny," I said.

"Are you watching?"

"Yeah. So what are they going to do, tear the place down? People broke their backs getting those stones and hauling them up that hill—"

"That hill was the least of their trials."

"Right. So you know what I mean. How can they just tear it down because it doesn't have plumbing?"

He was wiping his hands on a rag, and turned away from the bench. Apparently I had missed the whole process, but I could worry about that later.

"They're not tearing it down," he said.

"What?"

"They're not building up on the hill. It's not really a great lot for a church. It makes a good postcard, but people have to take those steps in all kinds of weather. They're looking into buying the lot where the old hardware store was."

"The old hardware store? Across the street from the strip mall? What are they thinking?" In the background we could hear my mother calling through the kitchen window that dinner was ready, and the aroma which must have been wafting under our noses the whole time finally ascended into awareness.

"What are you getting so worked up about? This is a good thing, Son. We'll have better parking, modern facilities."

"We could just run plumbing out to the old church."

"Son," he said like a firm grip of assurance, "come on in to dinner. We can talk about this later."

As I followed him along the stepping stone path to the back door, I spotted the outline of the stones upon the distant hill with a quick look over my shoulder. An agonizing, charred hand grasping for some solace from Heaven. But what comfort could come in the knowledge that we were abandoning the old God?

Separation of church and state can be smoothed over like a rolling stop at an obscure intersection in a small town. There were no other suitable enclosures large enough to seat a congregation, so the high school auditorium hosted our services until the new church was finished. My father would comment that at least the seats were padded, and Russ McGuire, whose daughter Amy's advances I dodged throughout much of high school, would add that it made for easier sleeping.

According to the program, there would be a special meeting after service to discuss the Board's decisions on the new church, so I convinced my dad to stick around, though Mom caught a ride home to start dinner.

"These past few weeks we've been investigating all sorts of options and plans," the director, Mr. Parsons, told us from the microphone at center stage. "As you know, we have purchased the downtown lot, and we expect a few estimates on the construction as soon as next week. Now, as for the matter of the old church, we think we have come up with a fabulous idea which will benefit the community—"

"And how much will it cost?" one of the older ranchers from the outskirts called up from behind us. "This new church is gonna drain the collection plate, and we ain't all millionaires."

"Well, that's one of the best parts of our plan. We looked into having the stones removed so we could sell the lot, but up there on that hill like that it was going to run so much we didn't expect to be able to turn a profit on the whole process. That's when we came up with our idea. Would you believe that if we cleaned the place up just a bit, and spent just enough for a few signs, that we would be able to get something back out of that behemoth, after all?"

When the clamor that Mr. Parsons had apparently intended to spark did not appear, he continued.

"We're thinking of turning the old church into a historical site. Something for people to stop and look at while they're in town. Just think about it. We have dozens of people each day in the summer driving through here on their way to someplace else that has something to look at. Now, this won't make us Sedona, or anything, but it might just keep people in town long enough to spend a few dollars. Maybe grab lunch, or even spend the night. All we've really got to do, like I said, is clean it up a bit and put up some signs and railings, and whatnot. That old pile of stones has the kind of history that tourists want to know about."

My skin itched to hear that what was the House of God a few weeks ago was now remembered as if it had always been a hindrance.

As soon as the Board had some figures to show around they held a town meeting to determine the final fate of the church. My dad wouldn't let me attend. "You can't vote, anyway," he explained, which I understood as his way of protecting me from disappointment. I knew as well as he that the Board's suggestions would be adopted almost without hesitation. Soon enough, ground broke on construction of the new church downtown, where they had an architect's sketch of the finished structure stapled onto a piece of plywood for folks to see.

In the meantime, there was a bronze plaque mounted onto a granite pedestal—somehow shaped like a tombstone—at the foot of the steps of the old church. A more detailed account of the history of the building, too long to be engraved in such ore, was featured inside a glass-enclosed bulletin board on the other side of the stairs, along with a black-and-white photo of the church before the fire.

I gave in to Amy McGuire's persistent notes in my locker and sweetly suggestive glances during class and started dating her in my junior year. We were never an item of the type that would be included on the Sweethearts Page of the yearbook, but she was full of the kind of fire a young man desires on Friday nights when there's no movie theater for thirty miles. Still, my mom periodically warned me about small town girls with C-plus averages. "I don't care what you do with your life," she would say, "but you be sure you do something with it before some girl with nothing to look forward to anchors you down."

But Amy and I were sort of like a part-time job. Actually, no. The job got more of my devotion. When summer came around, I stayed busy at Lincoln's station most of the time, and was too tired to flick a flea the rest of the time. I had bought myself an old Chevy C-10 that had been losing its luster under the sun, up on blocks out behind our neighbor's place, and spent most of my time and energy getting it running. It ran after just an oil change, but there was a lot of work to do to make it dependable. I wasn't concerned with a cherry red paint job or switching out for a 454 under the hood like the other guys my age, who spent hours just standing around talking about their wheels, had suggested. I had had my eyes on that truck since I was old enough to think about driving, but now had not only a license but a sense of purpose in buying the truck. Not for dating Amy. For the freedom of the road. When I borrowed my dad's truck, I wouldn't dare keep it out longer than necessary, as there was no telling when he might need it. But with my own vehicle, I could experience the sensation of a deserted highway in those cool-as-deep-water Arizona nights. Each excursion would take me farther, later than before. Those were the test runs for the truck-'s eventual mission, which had yet to be revealed even to me.

By the end of the summer, it was official. Cliffside's effort to attract tourism dollars had failed. Maybe not, some said. Maybe it was just going to take a little longer. Maybe folks noticed it this year, and would come back around to see it next year. But only a few cars stopped each day, and the money they spent in town didn't seem like any more than usual. Certainly not enough to repay the money already invested in transforming the old church into a historical landmark.

We could get ourselves onto the National Register of Historical Sites, someone suggested. But that would take too long. The Board was desperate to save face. And just when they needed it most, along came a way to do just that.

There had been one particular visitor, whom a few folks claimed to recall after his phone call to the mayor, who had truly admired the church. This fellow was a member of some historical society back in Virginia, and had taken a deep interest in our church because his organization sometimes located unique pieces for wealthy collectors. As it would happen, there was a tobacco magnate who had bought a historic plantation a few years before and had been patiently waiting for news of a centerpiece worthy of his gardens—which probably amounted to more acreage than downtown Cliffside.

The architectural style really wasn't that important, this Virginian said. Our church had a dominating presence like the Parthenon. He had been thinking along the lines of a fountain or a small menagerie of sculptures, but now he knew our church was the perfect piece. He had already shown the magnate the pictures.

Tobacco Man's money could have convinced the Board, if they had needed any persuasion.

"Are you crazy?" a few would ask. "How are you going to sell a church to someone in Virginia?"

"Now, you're forgetting that they moved the whole London Bridge down to Lake Havasu a few years back. We can certainly send this pile of stones. Anyway, he's paying for everything."

And that really was the bottom line, wasn't it? Money. We would sell heritage for a profit. And do what with the money? Spend it on a few stretches of asphalt that would need replaced in a decade? Some consolation for our posterity.

Watching over the peaks of pines from the gas station as the crane swooped back and forth along its arc, loading flat-bed trucks with the remains of our church was the catalyst to finally react with the ingredients I had accumulated. The truck I now understood like a prisoner understands a ring of skeleton keys hung within arm's reach of his cell.

I stopped seeing Amy altogether. Knowing I would be leaving soon, I also grew saucier with the customers who pulled up to the full-service pump. The part I regret is that I even treated Lincoln and his business with a ripening disdain that he didn't deserve.

The seldom Cadillacs that used to awe me as a child as they cruised our humble street had all but disappeared. Out-of-state Lexuses and Jeep Grand Cherokees—which not one of their drivers dared to take off-road—with the power windows up and the air conditioning cooling the cavernous interior behind the driver and sole passenger.

“You’d get better mileage if you rolled your windows down,” I said to one such driver. “These mountains put a lot of strain on your engine, and the air conditioning draws a lot of power.”

“Oh, we haven’t had any trouble,” he said. “If I punch it, this baby'll tear up any slope at seventy-five, even with the air on.”

“Still, you’re missing the best part of the drive: the fresh air.”

“We came over for a week. We’ll get plenty of fresh air at the lake.”

Over from California, according to the plates. Heading to a rental cabin, most likely. Anyhow, as I took his fifty inside for Lincoln to make change, I swiped a pine tree air-freshener from the cardboard display next to the register. Lincoln was too busy with the money to notice, and shouldn’t have minded, anyway. He sold maybe one of them a month at seventy-five cents each, which couldn’t have been a lot of profit.

“Something to remember us by,” I said, handing the little tree cut-out to the customer.

“I really don’t need it,” he said, turning it over in his hand as if the other side would be more exciting.

“Of course not,” I said. “All you have to do is roll down your windows and you’ll be bathed in the scent of the largest ponderosa pine forest in the world. But since you’re afraid our air is as bad as where you came from, this is the next best thing.”

Standing there stolidly to show I wouldn’t have minded if he marched inside to complain to Lincoln, I was relieved he didn’t, since it wasn’t the folks in Cliffside I wanted to offend.

You take for granted that the reason the young want to leave the nest is that they sense there is something out there waiting to be seen, something they can't find around home. You take for granted you know better, but know they'll suit themselves regardless. In my case, it was because we had had all that was ever sacred, and pawned it.

"And you don't know where you're headed?" my father confirmed even as I was hoisting my stuff over the side of the truck bed.

"Nope. Not really."

Hours after quitting with Lincoln I had told my parents that I would be leaving, allowing them the same two weeks' notice in which to question my intent.

" Well, that sounds like a real fine way to set out on life. Yessir."

He retreated to the porch, but stopped short of going inside. Eyes down, hands in pockets, he mumbled a curse, inspired by affection. As much as I wanted to drop my gear and go hug him, I was at the age when I understood why men should not cry, and I would no sooner have tempted him to do so where the neighbors could see him than embark on my own mission with red, swollen eyes. At least I was blessed with a mother with unfathomable insight who knew why it had to be this way, and could soothe him after I was gone.

"You know the number," she said. "Call collect if you have to, but let us know where you are, now and then."

"I will," I promised. She probably thought I'd be back in a week. I knew better.

In moments, I would be accelerating away from the only safe cove I had ever known, fearing I would never be able to find the road back, knowing that turning around even at that moment could not satisfy the swell within me. In the instant that you break your own heart like kindling over your knee and cast it behind you because of the discomfort of a single splinter—entangled with the decision to start anew rather than waiting to heal, you may appreciate the essence of love. If not, you have already succumbed to contempt.

This could be one of those tales with the son regretting he wasn't around when his father passed away; or with a hero who is not recognized when he returns from a decade of experiences to find his once-upon-a-time world shriveled too small to entertain his ambition. That remains to be seen. But it is one in which a character—I won't call myself a hero—sets out on a quest. He doesn't know just what for, or if it is only a myth, but knows that the drive to pursue it will never leave him at ease until he at least tries.

Interred With the Bones

Five houses, seven schools, three years. That was the track record of my father's search for the right job. His mother called him restless; his mother-in-law called him shiftless. At any rate, my father's restless lifestyle ended just before I entered the fourth grade. So much for change being the only constant.

We settled in a town with the unlikely name of Cliffside. End of the road. Having no idea that permanence was in the offing, it was business as usual when I started at Rutherford B. Hayes Elementary School: indifference regarding my identity from everyone in my class reciprocated by my own aloofness. Just another year of doodling during math, enjoying the seat at the back of the room that would keep me out of the spotlight. Falling through the cracks? More like scurrying into them.

When it became apparent that I wasn't going away as originally expected, my presence shifted along the spectrum from "resentful" right to "intolerable," and it was no longer enough to ignore me. Now I had to be shunned. The playground was malicious. I was singled-out during dodge-ball and they made sure I was one of the first to be hit. When teams were picked for baseball or kickball, I was left nudging stones along the playground perimeter, which scuffed the toes of my sneakers much more than kickball or soccer ever would. I wondered if I wanted to belong. When the bell rang, I let everyone out-run me to the stolid brick box which had become my prison instead of motel. I looked across the plains to the mill where my father worked and wished he was thinking the same thing about the town, and that by evening we would be moving on.

I had no delusions of making friends in that school. Nor did I yet have any inkling that the deepest friendship of my life would occur in that town.

At night I would hold my transistor radio up to my bedroom window in hopes of receiving my favorite radio program. Though there was plenty of adventure on TV, the radio serials launched my imagination in directions TV never could. But we had moved too far from the stations that broadcast the exploits of the Dark Night Avenger. I settled for Saturday morning reruns of black and white episodes of Flash Gordon. They beat anything on prime time, but not the Avenger.

That first year passed like gravel straining through an hourglass. But my summer parole from Hayes arrived with the promise of solace, and of finally making a friend.

Chad Palmer usually spent recess among the other kids, but only as the ribbon tied to the dragon's tail. He quietly took his turns at bat, while the outfielders saved their chatter for the big-shots. Though he was not part of the in-crowd, he was certainly not shunned, not seen as a burden. Actually, maybe he was a respite from themselves: a short recess from the recess in which everyone could rest in his mediocrity and not feel pressed to rave or brag for just one moment. You could count on Chad for a base hit, an occasional a triple. Never a home run or touchdown, though the story of his one amazing interception was carried back into the classroom as if the story itself were the hero on the shoulders of his teammates. Like everyone else who was not already a member, Chad seemed the perennial pledge, aspiring to belong.

So, though I was surprised to see him riding his bike along the sidewalk in front of Mr. Murdoch's house one day that first summer, it didn't seem odd that he was alone. He was coasting along aimlessly, letting his bike snake from side to side within the bounds of the sun-bleached concrete path. At first my plan was just to let him go by. Actually, I couldn't have imagined doing anything else, but then suddenly I did.

"Hey, Chad!" I said.

He snapped his head around and almost lost control of his bike. "Where are you?" he said.

"Up here." Already the conversation was verging on lengthy by my standards.

Straddling the frame of his bike, he tilted his head all the way back, looking almost straight up to see me. "What are you doing?" he asked.

I looked around to see for myself. "Just climbing, I guess."

Then he had one foot on his pedal, like he was getting ready to take off again, so I said abruptly, "Wanna come up?"

He looked up and down the street, but no one was coming or going. "All right," he said. I scooted out on the branch a little so he would have room to climb. "What are you doing up in this tree, anyway?" Chad asked when he was settled on a branch.

"What do you mean?"

"Well, it's not your tree. It's Mr. Murdoch's tree," he said. That was the first time that I had heard the name, or even cared whose tree it was.

"So?" I said.

"Well, it's just that my folks told me to stay away from Old Man Murdoch, so I figured maybe yours did, too."

"Nope," I said. "They've never said anything about him."

I looked through the leaves at the house's indifferent facade, picturing some phlegm-hacking, unbathed, crotchety old troll. But the brilliance of daylight diluted my imagination.

"Is he a criminal, or something?" I asked.

"No," Chad said. "I'm not sure exactly what's wrong with him, but my dad told me not to go near him."

"Aren't you curious, though?"

"Nah. Not really. I was when he first moved in, but now I see him at the store almost every week. He looks all right, but my dad still says to keep clear of him."

What could be so bad about the guy? Was he a leper, or something? And what was a leper? I was curious about Mr. Murdoch, but that could wait. At present, I was close to having a new friend—my first friend in a very long time—and that was more important than whatever mystery surrounded Mr. Murdoch.

"You live around here?" I asked.

"Sure. Right up the street. About two blocks over from your place."

"How do you know where… "

"Not too many people move here. I was watching when your family moved in," he said.

"Oh."

"Look, I better go before my dad drives by, or something. He'd kill me."

He swooped down and dropped near his bike.

"Well, if you want to, you can come over sometime," I said, "since you know where I live."

"All right," Chad said, already pumping his bike to cruising speed. Whether to distance himself from the forbidden zone or me, I didn't know. I could hardly recognize the faintly desperate sound of my own voice, but I knew that hollow implosion in my stomach. I didn't expect to see him again until school started.

Mr. Murdoch's tree had smooth, thin bark that didn't scratch my legs when I climbed it wearing shorts; and its trunk was just small enough, just rippled and gnarled enough, that I could shimmy to the lowest branches with just the sparsest spit rubbed between my palms—the soles of my monkey-like feet already tacky from sweating in sneakers without socks. So, shoes discarded in the plush grass, bike resting on its side, I climbed. The tree also had no fruit, which meant less bugs than apple or mulberry trees, and that there were no nuts to be painfully landed upon when dropping to the ground. So is it any wonder that my second home was above Mr. Murdoch's front lawn?

There were only a few times I recall seeing Mr. Murdoch, and only now wonder how many times he might have seen me: my tanned, soft skin swallowed by those fleshy leaves. How many times did he see me swoop out of that plush, green cloud, dangle from the lowest branch until my body nearly stopped swinging, then plop to the ground, stab my feet into my gritty shoes, and drag my bike to the sidewalk to burst home in time for dinner? How many times before the first day he called me to the porch?

Standing on the top step, with one hand lazily set on the railing at his side, the other hand in the air near his hip, waving me toward him with a grasping motion as he called gently, "Come here, boy."

As opossums dissemble death to defend themselves, I froze in my position. Did I expect my arms to appear as branches?

"Come on, now. I see you there."

"I'm sorry I'm in your tree," I said, hoping to circumvent whatever chastisement he was waiting to unleash.

"That's all right. It's not my tree, anyway. That's on city land. But won't you just come down here for a moment?"

Reluctantly, exercising more care with each foothold than usual, I descended. He must have ducked back inside for a moment, because now he held a pen and pocket-size notepad, on which he was writing. For all the talk of old Mr. Murdoch, he was not so old, standing there in a pair of casual khaki pants, and a navy polo shirt. At the time I guessed his age to be forty, and was not far off. About halfway up the walkway to his porch, I paused.

"Here, now," he said, finishing writing. "Do you know where the drug store is?"

"Yes, Sir," I said.

"Well, then, if you have a moment, I was wondering if you could do me a favor. I'll pay you."

He seemed to be waiting for my acceptance before informing me of the nature of the favor, so I nodded my head.

"Good. I need you to get me some India ink. They have it in little black jars in the stationery section. If you can't find it, just ask the clerk. It should be a few dollars. You get that, and you can have the change," he said, tearing the note from the pad, handing it to me with a five dollar bill on top. I moved the money to read the note. "India Ink," it said, underlined twice.

"Well, get going, now. I need that right away."

I plunged the cash and note into the pocket of my cut-offs, then grabbed my handlebars and ran with my bike a few steps before leaping on like a cowboy onto a moving horse.

Though Cliffside was a small town, houses dotted the hills in the distance. Still, the entire population could dance on the high school football field simultaneously. Our house and Mr. Murdoch's were just a few blocks behind Main Street, a mile-long 30 mile-per-hour zone of the highway that bisected the town, along which the businesses formed a single commercial corridor. Since there were no stoplights in town back then, you just had to put a foot, or front bicycle tire, into the crosswalk in front of the post office, and the locals would come to a stop for you. I leaned my bike against the front exterior wall of the drugstore and went directly inside to the stationery section, where I found a column of squatty black bottles sporting the label "India Ink."

"You're not giving yourself a tattoo, are you?" the clerk asked before reading the price into the cash register. I wasn't sure if she was lightly suspicious and mostly kidding, or the other way around. When I became older, I would be interrogated in much the same fashion every time I tried to buy alcohol.

"No," I said. I had no idea you could do such a thing. "It's for Mr. Murdoch."

"Mr. Murdoch?" she said, with a surprise which you wouldn't call pleasant evident in her voice.

"He asked me to get it for him."

"All right," she said, turning to the register. "That's three-o-five."

Though I was ecstatic at the idea of making almost two dollars for something so simple, I withstood the temptation to head back to the candy bar rack at that instant, fearing I had misunderstood Mr. Murdoch. Who would pay two dollars for such an easy errand? But when I dropped my bike on the grass strip between the sidewalk and street and leapt up the steps to his porch and he answered the door just before I could knock, he didn't even put out a hand to receive the change that I extended toward him.

"That's yours," he said. "Thank you very much."

He waited, as if to see me off, as I waited, partially dumbstruck by the reality of my wage, and also hoping to peer inside and see whether there were a client waiting for a tattoo in his living room. Mr. Murdoch stepped backward through the threshold, his free hand blindly reaching behind him and finding the edge of the door, curling behind that to the knob on the inside. But before he sealed himself in, he said, "What's your name, son?"

"Matt," I said.

Without his eyes leaving my face, the door swooped to rest against the jam.

"Where'd you get that money?" Dad asked, seeing me counting my bounty on the front porch after dinner.

"Mr. Murdoch gave it to me for running an errand for him," I said.

"Murdoch? Who's that? Your teacher?"

"No. He's just a guy who lives around here."

"Well, what did he pay you to do? Mow his lawn?"

"No. I just went to the store and got some India ink for him," I said, proud to know what India ink was.

"And he paid you a dollar?"

"Almost two dollars," I said. "He told me to keep the change, and it was only three-o-five for the ink. So I got a dollar ninety-five."

The rest of the evening, my dad seemed to be trying to solve the mystery of the money I had, though there should have been no mystery at all. He asked my mom who Mr. Murdoch was, but she didn't know. Then he and she each counted, and re-counted together the grocery money in the sugar jar above the sink. Finally, about an hour and a half after the conversation on the porch, Dad called me into the living room and told me to sit on the sofa. He sat on the edge of his chair at the end of the sofa, hands folded, leaning on his forearms across his knees.

"Matthew," he said, "I only want to ask you this once, so I want you to tell me the truth."

There he paused, as if to confirm that I understood, so I nodded.

"Matt, where did you get that money? Did you steal it from somewhere?"

"Mr. Murdoch gave it to me," I said, confused. Why didn't he believe me?

"I just find it hard to believe that someone would give you two dollars just to run to the store and spend three dollars. It doesn't make sense. Now, I hope that I've taught you better than to steal—or to lie to me."

"I'm not lying. Really. Mr. Murdoch told me to keep the change. I even tried to give it back to him, but he wouldn't take it."

"All right, Matt," he said after a minute. But he sighed when he did, letting me know he was not satisfied. Later, after being sent to bed, I could hear him and Mom talking, and remember him saying, "Well, if he didn't get it out of the sugar jar, where could he have taken it from?"

The irony of that evening would not come out until I was in high school.

I was hesitant to get too excited the next time Chad pedaled by me as I loafed in Mr. Murdoch's tree. Still, he parked his bike of his own accord when he saw mine leaning against the trunk. Much to my surprise, Chad and I began to hang out, literally, more and more often in that tree in front of Mr. Murdoch's house. Sure, there were other trees around. But most of them had trunks far too wide and high to climb without slinging a rope over the lowest branch. Besides, in this tree there was always the suspense of Mr. Murdoch and his secret lair.

"What's he do in there all day long?" I asked Chad.

"Don't you know? He's an artist."

Not old enough to envision the canon of works which would be taught to me as "Art" in college, nothing more than an abstract jumble of brushes and smocks and the image of a painter, thumb poking through a palette populated with heavy dollops of oil paints, a beret and fine mustache decorating his head, came to mind. Before I could solicit any details, Chad volunteered more.

"He draws super-heroes. My dad says he's queer."

The two juxtaposed statements refused to be reconciled by my understanding.

"Superheroes," I said, attaching more importance to that detail. "Like who?"

"Oh, he has his own comic. Captain Valor."

"Is it famous?"

"I don't know. You can buy it at the drugstore."

And so I did. I used some of the money Mr. Murdoch had given me and I bought issue number forty-two of Captain Valor. Hours, I spent studying the pictures whose dynamic features it seemed miraculous to constrain to a simple, flat piece of paper. For the first time, it seemed that someone else had the same imagination as mine. These were drawings worthy of the Dark Night Avenger. These were the forms and motions that had played in my mind. More than anything, I wanted to learn the secrets of this magic. This transcription of wonder.

Using more of the money to buy a pad of typing paper, I traced the cover image, and then the more exciting poses from inside. Still, my renditions were clumsy, like a wooden doll carved with a dull hatchet next to a streamlined, stainless-steel robot. Since I had gotten that first issue in the middle of the month, I only had to wait a few weeks to get the next issue. In the meantime, I also borrowed back-issues from Chad, who told me, "Keep 'em."

To say the least, I was fascinated by the flashy costumes and explosive battles: costumed titans who toppled factories and hurled semi-trucks through the air as effortlessly as a paperboy slinging the news. But it was page four of issue forty-four, which came out just more than a week before school resumed, that truly astonished me. There, clear as a mirror reflection, was my face, drawn in ink. The comic book boy's name was Matt, just like me. Atop his building's roof to stargaze one evening, Matt spied Captain Valor cruising through the sky to light on a neighboring rooftop. When Captain Valor saw that his secret identity was in jeopardy, he made a pact with Matt to always protect his secret.

I hadn't spoken to Mr. Murdoch since running his errand, but I felt entitled, seeing as I had appeared in his comic. So, comic book in hand (as if I might need proof), I timidly approached his door.

"What is it?" he called from a back room in response to my knock. Not knowing what to say, I simply knocked again. Finally, he answered the door. "Oh, you. What's that? You want me to sign it for you, or something?"

"No. You drew me." Even I didn't know if it was with accusation or appreciation that I spoke.

"So I did. And I thought I might do it again. After all, you've been scampering in and out of my tree all summer, why not find your way into my pages?"

"You said it isn't your tree."

"Well, you've got me," he said, and I saw a smile almost crack across his face. "You got me. So, what do you want?"

Nothing beyond the initial acknowledgment had been foreseen in my thinking. I suppose I had just expected him to confirm that it was me who he had drawn, and then I would turn around and leave. But, standing there, an opportunity seemed to present itself, and I frantically sought to determine what it might be.

"I draw, too," I said.

"Is that so? What do you draw?"

"Your pictures. I have almost ten of your comics at home, and I've been practicing drawing your pictures. I trace them, sometimes, but I can just look at them and draw them, too."

It was true. In a span of several weeks, I had begun to develop the rudimentary skills of an artist.

"Is that so?" Mr. Murdoch said. Then, almost as if he were speaking over my shoulder to someone standing behind me, he said, "I'm surprised you can even buy my comic books in this town." He again focused his speech at me, saying, "Why don't you bring your drawings by sometime? I'd like to see them."

With that, he retreated back into his home, and I practically drug my bike behind me as I tore down the street toward home. I dashed upstairs, dropped the comic on my bed, and snatched my drawing pad from the top of my dresser. When I knocked on Mr. Murdoch's door again, I was huffing for air after my super-sonic relay. He must have recognized the knock, because he didn't yell, just opened the door.

"What? What is it?"

"I brought my drawings," I said between gasps.

"Now? I didn't mean right now."

Whether it was my zeal or a pang of pity that changed his mind, I'll never know, but he reconsidered. "Well," he said, "I guess you're here, so why don't you come in and let's take a look at what you've got."

"You've been inside his house?" Danny Briggs asked. Danny and Brad Watson were the gods of my grade. Where they went, others aspired to be. So nearly the whole class was in train like a dust cloud kicked up by their heels as they approached me across the playground. Chad was right off Brad's flank, so I could tell he had sold his first-hand knowledge of my first-hand experience for a few moments of acknowledgment.

"So, has he got robots or super-hero costumes or stuff like that?" someone else asked out of turn.

"Shut up," Brad called behind him, amassing a small avalanche of rebuke from the others toward the unseen speaker.

"Nah. He's just got a den for drawing. You know, drafting tables and stuff. Except for that, it's just a normal place with a sofa and easy chair and TV set," I said, aiming to disappoint them. If they were going to accept me, it wasn't going to be due to mad scientist stories about Mr. Murdoch. That one short exchange on the playground did not prove to be the beginning of acceptance for me, and despite my maturing disdain for social ladders, I did not wish to be the bottom rung. Though a few families moved into town every year, none of them seemed to have kids my age, which meant for years I would be known to my classmates as "the new kid."

In the meantime, I dared to knock on Mr. Murdoch's door whenever I had finished a new drawing, which I increasingly spent more time and attention on. Never underestimate the natural force that an audience has on children's development. Mr. Murdoch's first critique of my work was limited to mentioning that I had merely copied his drawings, but showed some talent. In the future, I tried my best not to copy his comics, but where else in the world could I find models of super-heroes to depict? Other comics had the whole spectrum of colors, but none were imbued with the efficient power of strokes which defined Captain Valor.

As we grew comfortable with each other, I used the pad of drawing paper Mr. Murdoch had given me to sketch scenes right there in his den as he worked at the drafting table on wide drawing boards of Captain Valor. It was understood that I could not tell anyone else what I saw him committing to paper: an agreement I honored without exception. When he took coffee breaks he would call me along into the living room, which was furnished just as I had told my schoolmates. There, sipping from his mug, he would hold my pad up to face level in one hand to regard what I was working on. Over the years his comments on my drawings would always acknowledge what I had mastered and challenge me to refine my skills one step further.

Eventually, we reached a mature and sometimes mutual exchange of minute scrutiny over every elbow and ear lobe on our pages.

"How did you learn to draw skyscrapers?" I once asked Mr. Murdoch, noting that there were no such buildings around to be studied.

"I lived in some bigger cities when I was younger," he said.

"So why did you move to Cliffside?"

"Well, I didn't, at first. My father was diagnosed with tuberculosis, so he moved us out here to Phoenix, because the doctor said the dry climate would be the best treatment. I lived down there while I finished high school, then went back to Kansas City to start art school. Then it was off to New York to start work at the comic book company. Got married there, and divorced, too. So when I got the chance to launch my own title, I decided to move back home, as it were. But Phoenix was growing up too fast, so I came up here."

It hadn't really dawned on me before that how much living a person might have to go through to end up in here. But here wasn't such a bad place to be. Even my dad had settled and found success as the mill's financial officer. We moved into a new, larger house, though only a block away from the first, and didn't even bother trading in the old truck on the Cherokee. But my dad wasn't the only industrious member of the family. Bored at home, my mom opened up a video rental store before anyone else in town realized what a shrewd move it would prove to be.

Still, I got neither acceptance from my classmates nor my parents. My classmates were tickled to find that "Matt" had become a regular character in the comic, and tried different names on me until they decided "Wonder Boy" had the most condescending ring to it. As for my parents, my dad wanted me to work after school at the video store so my mom wouldn't have to hire any extra help. It wasn't all that bad because we were never too busy before mid-evening, so I had plenty of time to sketch the patrons as they lazily browsed the titles. It was like having a free gallery of models, always changing costumes, poses, bodily features. People browsing the shelves of a video store are far more animated than you might suspect. Their expressions are either determined by the fact that they haven't considered someone might be watching them, or that they are positive someone is. Now and then someone would spy me working on them, and I would show the sketch, if they asked. Some I signed and gave away. Others took turns in the front window, which my mom tried to convince my dad that the customers adored.

But my dad was not so enamored with my talents or my acquaintance with Mr. Murdoch. When Mr. Murdoch gave me a posable statue attached to a base to help me learn to draw the human form more naturally, my dad picked it up for inspection as if it were a voodoo doll.

"Now what the hell is this for?" he said.

"It's a figure for drawing. You just position it—"

"I don't mean that. I mean what did he give it to you for?"

I had no clue what he might be insinuating.

"What does he have you doing over there with him? That's what I mean. Does he get dressed up in his blue tights? The guys out at the mill told me all about your friend Mr. Murdoch. Some kind of Peter Pan fairy who likes little boys."

He couldn't have been more wrong. In fact, I doubt if he actually believed it himself, but he was worried about something, and worry can make you latch onto the most absurd of ideas. Yes, I had heard it, too. From the kids at school, and even one teacher who held me behind after class to ask me if Mr. Murdoch ever touched me. For the record, no. Never, not once, not at all. It was just the town's way of explaining why there was a single man staying indoors all day drawing super-heroes. It's much easier to imagine the monster's form in the dark than to turn on the light and dissipate those horrible imaginings.

The proudest moment of my adolescent life was not a game-winning home run in the ninth inning, nor taking the prettiest girl in school to the homecoming dance. It was in late February of my sophomore year, and Mr. Murdoch was finishing issue #112 of Captain Valor. I still spent as much of my free time as possible working in his den, and as my talent and our friendship had grown, so had the popularity of his comic. He now had a schedule of convention appearances that dragged him all over the country for several days at a time. So it was not surprising that upon returning from Chicago he came down with a bad flu and could barely stay awake, much less sit upright at the drafting table and complete the comic on time. But he had already penciled the whole story board, and had inked all but the last seven pages. So all that was left was to ink in those final pages, and send the black and white artwork to the company, where someone else had taken over the coloring duties, in light of Mr. Murdoch's hectic schedule.

"What the hell are you doing, Matthew?" he tried to bark through his wheezing lungs when he wandered into the den to find me working on the ink.

"Well, I knew you wouldn't be able to finish in time, so I thought I would just help you out."

"Matthew, if you mess up any of these boards, I'll have to start from scratch."

But I knew he could start from scratch and do the whole thing over again in a few hours, when he was healthy. In fact, by that time, so could I. The hardest part was coming up with the angles for the reader's viewpoint, and the placement of the characters in the frame. But he had already taken care of that, so the rest was like tracing—but more intricate.

"Don't worry," I said, putting my brush into the India ink. "Why don't you just go rest, and let me take care of this?"

But he lingered there, hunched under a thick blanket which he hugged around himself, hands hidden within its comfort. Then he brought one hand out to lift aside an inked page and look at the other underneath. It was my work, but not even he could tell it from his. I had been his understudy for nearly six years at that point.

"All right," he said, his hand regathering the blanket toward his throat. "You know where to send them?"

"I know. The address is right there on the bulletin board. Don't worry. I'll show them to you before I wrap them up, all right?"

"I don't know how to thank you, son," he said.

After that, Mr. Murdoch made a point of letting me do a little work on each issue, not because he was lazy or falling behind, but as a condition of my apprenticeship. When issue #112 hit the stands I wished there were someone else I could share my secret with, much as Captain Valor had felt from time to time. Over the years, Matt had grown up along with me, and had developed almost into a side-kick. So at least the Captain had Matt to confide in. And at least Mr. Murdoch and I understood each other. Because the time was approaching when friends would grow even more scarce than ever.

The trouble arrived in waves, like reinforcements to an original onslaught. First was the City Council. Then the mill. And then the worst of them all. But one at a time.

Mr. Murdoch didn't think much of the City Manager, and so he didn't think much of the visit which the manager requested. He was working in his rolled-up sleeves until the knock came at the door, then leaving me to sketch in the den alone as he welcomed the manager and a few others into his living room. No door was hung on the jam between the den and living room, so I had an unobstructed view of them all, sitting side-by-side on his couch, the heavy, drawn drapes behind them. He didn't even turn on a light. I could draw the scene from memory even now. But I tried not to seem as if I were spying, so mostly just listened and pretended to be engulfed in the drawing before me. Still, this is the essence of what they said:

"Mr. Murdoch, it's nice to finally meet you."

"Well, I've been in seclusion."

"Yes, well, let me get right to the point. Your little comic has turned into quite an enterprise, am I right?"

I didn't look to see his expression as Mr. Murdoch refrained from answering.

"Well," the manager continued, "the people of Cliffside feel truly honored to have such a celebrity in their midst, and we have developed a plan of mutual benefit for you and the town. What we would like to do is—"

"Since when?" Mr. Murdoch interrupted.

"Excuse me?" the manager said.

"Since when have the people of Cliffside felt honored at my presence?"

"Well, always. We've always thought of you as one of our own, of course."

"Is that so?"

"An adopted son," one of the other voices said.

"Exactly. And what we have planned is to erect a statue—of Captain Valor—in the park."

"There's a whole package, really," the third voice said. "We'd start by having new signs put out on the highway with Captain Valor welcoming visitors to Cliffside. 'Cliffside: Home of Captain Valor.' Then there's the statue, of course. And we would also like to start a little tour. Maybe once a day. The visitors could come and take a picture of you while you're working, and you could sign some autographs. We've looked into it, and we think this could give the town the little boost that it needs right now."

"You think people would drive thirty miles from the interstate to look at a statue of a comic book hero?"

"There's a town up in Canada that's done just about the same thing, and the local businesses have seen a measurable increase in their sales. You know, people go out of their way to see the oddest things. Giant balls of yarn, and stuff like that."

Mr. Murdoch paused before speaking, but knowing his tone of voice, I knew he was not actually considering their proposal. "There are issues of license to be wrangled over, you know."

"Yes, of course. We have already contacted the comic book company, and they informed us that you retain all rights to your characters. So we came to you."

"After going to the company in New York, then you came to me? Then you came to your adopted son?"

"Mr. Murdoch," the manager said, "please, don't be upset about that. That seemed the appropriate official route."

"Are you sure it wasn't just that you didn't want to talk to me? Maybe you were afraid that if you looked into my eyes I'd cast a spell over you and molest you?"

"Mr. Murdoch, please!"

"No. You listen. I know what you people think of me. And I also remember how many people before this have knocked on my door to visit me. One. I don't owe this town anything, and I will not give it anything."

"We really wish you would reconsider—"

"Gentlemen, thank you for your heartfelt offer, but I really have to be getting back to work."

With that he showed them out, standing in the doorway long enough to see them pull away. Not long afterwards, I saw the faces of the City Manager and his associates again. This time they were a band of three sinister but incompetent villains whom the Captain mopped up within four pages.

Mr. Murdoch's reaction might seem a bit indignant, but it wasn't you constantly shunned and avoided. It was him. It was me. He recognized that the representatives of the whole community would never be his captive audience again, on his own turf, and he took his shot. I can't blame him.

When I was younger, no one dared speak of the rumors to my face, though I'm sure those guys at the mill warned my dad. By the time I was in high school, people started to hold me accountable for my own decisions, and that included my relationship with Mr. Murdoch. To fend off the gossip, I even tried to start a relationship with a girl I met one time when I went with my mom to the JC Penny's thirty miles away. I mean, no girl in Cliffside would dare to even brush against me, so when I met Diana in the aisle between the boys' jeans and the girls' blouses, I made sure to get her phone number, even though I wasn't really attracted to her. But high school basketball games are rumor mills, and someone made it a point to tell her about me—whatever they were telling about me.

At least it was an enlightened age. A few centuries ago they would have burned us at a stake to satisfy their ignorance.

My father may have thought he was protecting me by not telling me what everyone else in town had already heard from their fathers or confirmed with the newspaper, but he was only setting me up for the worst day of my life. The other kids could not have been more pleased that it was my father who was accused of embezzling from the mill. On that day, taunts and nicknames gave way to sticks and stones, and I was beat up in turn by everyone bigger than me in the whole school, it seemed. Those smaller than me took shots while others held my arms behind my back.

Back at home, soaking in a tub instead of trying to apply ice to every bruise, I listened to my father's tardy explanation through the bathroom door.

"I was going to tell you," he said, "but I didn't want you to worry about it."

"Worry about it?" I would have said if it didn't hurt to talk. "You must have known that every other kid with a father working at the mill you screwed would be looking for revenge. You should have let me worry about it."

When there was a lull in eggs being slung at our front door and car horn expletives, my mom insisted that I go to the hospital to get x-rays. Nothing broken. But neither did the doctor who relied on the paychecks from the mill workers give me anything for the pain. Still, as I said earlier, the worst was yet to come.

When Mr. Murdoch received the letter, he retained his composure, though his disgust was evident.

"Can you believe this? Those greedy bastards are suing me to use the Captain Valor name and image in brochures and on those stupid town signs," Mr. Murdoch told me. "I spend my life working for something, and they think they have the right to it? What did they ever contribute?"

He wasn't upset about having to "share." I knew even then about the scholarships he funded for economically disadvantaged art students, not to mention the charity art auctions to benefit children's wards and orphanages. And I saw the heaps of fan-mail which were delivered to him every week, so I knew the extent to which he had given of himself to help others have hope. He opened his home and heart to me, and would have done the same for that whole treacherous town had they once asked. But instead, they eschewed him for a decade, coming to call only when they wanted to turn a profit off him. And now they would use the courts to wrench an undeserved booty from him. The image of Captain Valor writhing to escape the shackles of Dr. Detesto's power siphon came to mind. Mr. Murdoch would never have turned away anyone in need. But Cliffside wasn't in need: it had dollar signs in its eyes.

Mr. Murdoch set his lawyer to work, telling him to relay a simple message to the plaintiffs: "If you win in court, I'll up and leave your town and build a ten-acre museum to Captain Valor right down the street from Disneyland."

But when they won use of the image on their signs and in their brochures a few months later, Mr. Murdoch did not leave town. Perhaps he would have, but a new factor had entered the equation.

My father spent my senior year in prison. In a way, so did I. The leniency shown toward him was the effect of a bargain my father made to pay back all of the money, with interest, plus penalties. The other part of the bargain was that they not seize the video store or the house or car, as my mother still needed to provide for me. But everything was re-mortgaged or re-financed to begin repaying the funds my father had drained from the mill.

I took to staying home from school, not because of emotional distress caused by my father's incarceration, as the school counselor feebly postulated to my mother in a letter I intercepted before she came home from work. I just had no intention of being pulverized whenever someone felt the fancy. Even Chad, who had been the only kid to regularly talk to me of his own free will, kept his distance then. He never went so far as to throw a punch, but it hurt just the same when his arms helped hold me down for someone else to strike.

Anyway, I needed to work on my art skills if I intended to get into a school with a good art department.

"The police came to see me today," Mr. Murdoch said. He had been telling me to call him by his first name for some time, but it would never catch on.

"Oh yeah?"

"They must think I've finally gone and done something they can put me away for."

"Were they looking for me?"

"Or parts of you, I suppose."

"Sorry."

"Don't be. I've been dying to show someone what I've done with the place," he joked.

I went to the den to lay out the work I had brought with me for him to critique. I was building a portfolio. But Mr. Murdoch remained in the living room, saying, "Matt, come out here for a moment, won't you?"

"What's up?" I said, plopping down on the couch. He sat in his recliner, as usual, though without any coffee on the table at his side.

"Matt, I have something to tell you. I know you can handle this like an adult, so I'm just going to say it. Matt, I found out that I have cancer."

Oddly, those words were simultaneously ominous and empty. Of course, cancer was supposed to be bad, but he hardly looked like he was dying, so the gravity of the diagnosis refused to sink in. I tried to look solemn, but I guess all I managed was a blank stare. It was like a riddle I couldn't wrap my mind around. We talked through the night, and in many ways I found out more about him that night than the last seven years had allowed. He told stories of his wife, the dreams they had shared for a moment, and the devastation of a young divorce when he thought he was on top of the world. I told him of the girl in class I had had a crush on for four years. He talked of the starving days in college and his first show, and how it was a tremendous flop, and how his work in comic books started. He told me that he thought I had what it takes. Had more of it than he had had, he said. And maybe that was the point when I realized I was crying. We were trying to pack decades of man-to-man talks into one night because we both knew that those decades would never arrive.

Cancer. There was nothing we could do.

We woke in the early afternoon of the next day and foraged through the kitchen, only to settle on cold pizza. Mr. Murdoch was all business, chewing the pizza with its coagulated toppings. "Matt, I want you to help me with something. I don't know how much strength I'm going to have in the coming months, and there's something I need to take care of."

"Just name it," I said, knowing he couldn't possibly ask too much.

"You have to help me kill Captain Valor."

"Matthew, you have got to get yourself back to school," my mom feebly demanded. She was growing haggard as the father, the mother, the worker, and the homemaker. With the hours demanded of a video store operator, we rarely had dinner together unless I picked up take-out deli sandwiches and joined her behind the counter. I wished I could have taken up more of the load for her.

"Mom," I said, with no intent of disrespecting her if she would respect me, "I know school's important, but there's something I have to take care of now. I'll stay behind a year, or go to summer school, but I have to do this now."

"Is this something to do with Mr. Murdoch?" she asked without the degree of accusation others used when they said his name.

"Yes, it is. And I know you might think comic books are a waste of time, or that Mr. Murdoch is a strange man, or whatever, but he's my best friend, and he needs me to help him through something. All right?"

Perhaps my sense of melodrama has rewritten the memory of that exchange to fit into the panels of a comic, but the truth is there was little she could have done to stop me. I'm glad she didn't try, because there was not a part of me that wanted to become a bad son. I would visit my father on alternating weekends, ridding my heart of as much resentment as possible before sitting across the dividing glass from him. But he would be free someday, and we would have the next few decades to work things out between us. The only true friend of my childhood, on the other hand, would soon… it was like watching his family load the U-Haul, and knowing we wouldn't write letters.

We launched our attack over a six-month span of issues, to capitulate in a double-sized finale which promised the thousands of avid readers an unbelievable ending. It was advertised and hyped in a media blitz bigger than some Hollywood movies enjoy.

The comic book company already had two issues in advance, so we had a little time to work with. We needed to plot the whole six issues as if it were one novel. This was to be his masterpiece—though he never put it that way—and no publisher's deadline would rush it. We spent the first few days just deciding which characters to bring into the story, and what scenes they would play. Of course, we had to work some action into every issue, too, so the readers would get their fix and come back for more. After that, the story started to fill itself in, and layout work on the first issue was underway. Mr. Murdoch did the pencils and I inked them. But instead of sending these to the company for coloring, Mr. Murdoch resumed that duty himself, showing me his technique as he worked. The crowning glory was the cover artwork. It was as if a new range had been discovered in the spectrum: colors which solidified muscles and energized plasma blasts.

Unlike in the past, when I had anonymously inked a few pages for my own education, this was a real job, with my name going on the first page right next to Mr. Murdoch's. Work went terrifically fast, actually, and we had all six issues done in less than three months. In the meantime, the first of them was on sale, with demand surpassing the print run.

The story line could be summarized like this: after years of fighting crime and using his powers for the benefit of mankind, Captain Valor faces his most formidable challenge in the emergence of a new super-villain, Nemecide, whose powers seem unsurmountable. For the first three months, the Captain takes his lumps, lucky to escape with his life by the end of the third issue. But in their next confrontation, the Captain senses a possible weakness in his foe. All this time, lost loves and non-super-hero friends are woven into the narrative with a deftness never before seen in comics. Reviewers would defy the categorization of these last six issues as comics, proclaiming a new standard in the industry.

All the while that the Captain is fighting Nemicide he seems to be struggling to summon the strength needed to fight. By the end of the fifth issue, the reader will learn that all this time the Captain's own powers have been killing him. Poisoning him with radiation. So when the double-sized sixth and final issue in this saga, and in the history of Captain Valor, arrives on the racks every comic book fan in America knows the dilemma that he will face: use his powers to save the world from Nemicide, or stop using his powers and save himself. And we all know that although the woman he had always hoped to marry now knows his secret identity and reveals her love to him Captain Valor will not deliberate long on the matter before launching himself into one final round of mortal combat.

There is one secret that the readers would not be pre-cognizant of, however. The comic book company was contractually bound to not reveal the fate of Captain Valor. So the day that the final issue hit the stands, no one was prepared for the good guy to lose. True, the Captain defeated Nemicide. But the tremendous exertion of his powers cost him his own life.

People were upset. There were man-on-the-street interviews on the news network. The last page of the comic, however, told it all. It was an open letter to the readers, thanking them warmly for their support, and explaining why Mr. Murdoch felt compelled to control the fate of his own creation as his own fate was being decided by his Creator.

When the publicist and reporters called to request interviews, Mr. Murdoch could not be reached for comment. He had died two months before the final issue was released.

Shakespeare observed centuries ago, "The evil that men do lives after them;The good is oft interred with their bones." Still, I wonder if his insight wasn't only surface deep. That year my father spent in prison must have been just enough for his evil deeds to be forgotten, because the community accepted my father back into the fold with a party at the mill—of all places—upon his parole. He has passed on now, but the video store still has a virtual monopoly, so my mother remains in Cliffside, where I visit her once a year, or so.

My mother would say only one thing at my father's funeral: "He was always a good provider."

That's what we have agreed to remember about him. His family never went hungry. His son always had decent clothes and the furniture wasn't run-down. That's my father. That's what remains of him. What became of his hobbies or his dreams or his failures? Well, I guess we just looked at the whole pile and said somewhere silently, Hell, we can't go carrying around all that, and we chose the easiest, most pleasant, most satisfying kernel and swallowed that, and it's in us now. Sure, we can sift through the other memories when we have a quiet afternoon. But when we have only a moment, everything is contained in that one phrase which we can recite like the caption below a famous man's bust. It's the kind of thing you put on a tombstone to convince all those who never met him that he really was worth meeting and that their lives are all the less fulfilled for not having been there to see him. It's that one picture out of the whole crackling album that everyone could agree had favorable lighting and showed his best side and captured the sparkle in his eyes and the simultaneous frivolity and frugality in his grin.

It must have been a compromise between selective memory and charitable forgetfulness, because my father's most noteworthy deeds were hardly saint-like.

As for Mr. Murdoch, he had never truly wronged anyone that I know of, but it feels like there is a whole town that reviles him to this day. I suppose the people of Cliffside have forgotten about him by now, but when he died there was no memorial service for him there. I accompanied the body to Scottsdale, where his mother still lived, for a private funeral. It was his mother who informed me of a final secret that Mr. Murdoch had withheld from my confidence. In his will, I was given control of everything related to Captain Valor, which included the royalty checks which would pour in from t-shirts and dolls for years to come. Still, when I was approached to reincarnate the character, and with movie offers, I declined out of respect for Mr. Murdoch.

My credits in those last six issues, along with the fact that people in the business would come to recognize me as "Matt" from the comic, gave me a pretty good start in the comic book industry when I skipped art school and moved straight to New York. But my work is darker, less hopeful than the days of Captain Valor. Nostalgic as I am for the first few years of innocence in which I submerged myself into those epic battles where the good guys always won, I can not pretend that they will ever return. The world has changed. Or maybe the surface has been skimmed of some artificial colors and sweeteners we had stirred in long ago to combat the true bitterness, but which separated over time.

The Fabled Country Band
Fresh out of Cliffside, Arizona,
Unaware They Were Doomed to Self-Destruct

They will know that every last name branded in magic marker across a strip of masking tape belongs to a father who was once young and thought he'd just work the overtime for a year and save enough to get out for good. Those names in all capital letters seeming to be the very resin which keeps the tape from curling any farther upon itself from its hastily ripped ends and falling to the ground. They will know this town will hold them in like a black hole can capture light if they ever once don steel-toed Caterpillar boots and step into that molding mill. Musical talent will be merely a consequential coincidence. They will not know all their adolescent years as they sharpen their skills that this will present the very means of escape they have tried to conceive of. Nor that it will be the very dragon which turns them against each other.

They will be born and raised in that town, the smell of ponderosa pine like incense emanating from their fathers' Wrangler jeans; their mothers' voices calling from the living room, "Keep practicing! Another twenty minutes!"

Though they will have known each other all their lives, it won't be until middle school music class that they take notice of each others' talents, and not until their sophomore year in high school, all three of them in the same grade, that they get the notion to start a band. So they'll meet over in Blain's garage twice or three times a week for a few months, at first, not sure what the point of it all is, but heeding the hunch that something can be made out of all of this just the same. It'll take that long until they finally start to read each other, to hear each other, and then they will notice that they are getting good.

A schedule of practices at least four days a week will be adhered to fervently for the next two years, and not a one of them will mind, because when you're in prison the best thing you can do is make the time go faster. And if that happens to be done by sharpening the instrument of your deliverance, all the more satisfying.

Dusty, the drummer, will say one day in their senior year, "We've gotta audition for the homecoming dance."

"What? You know they always have Dwayne Tucker's band play the dance," Ely will say. Ely will play the bass. A good bass player. Only real music fans appreciate the character a good bass beat brings to a song.

"Ely, come on. If we can play the dance, it'll be our first gig. I mean, we're too young to play the bars, and the pastor don't want no country comin' from his pulpit. This is the only gig we can do right now."

Ely will look over at Blain, fiddling with his guitar, briefly looking up to flash his confident smile and give a thumbs up, then agree.

They'll put together a set of covers ranging the biggest hits of the last few years and a couple of classic country songs for good measure, take the auditions by storm, and ride out with the prize of playing that dance, plus the four hundred dollars the gig pays, leaving Dwayne Tucker and his band with a sour note ringing in their ears in the process.

"We nailed it!" Blain will shout once back in the garage.

"Yeah, but now we gotta round up another hour and a half of music to play. And play it good. This could be the only gig we ever see," Ely will say, the world outside Cliffside too distant to bank on, too big to trust, too wide to imagine they could succeed in it.

But they will put that set together. They will rehearse and hone their skills in the next few weeks with the dedication of Olympic athletes, knowing this comet won't come around again for a lifetime long time. So when Dusty breaks the tedium by smashing into uncharted drum solos, Ely will tear a sourly evil howl across his bass, and bark, "We ain't got time for that, Dusty! The dance's only a week away, man. Knock that shit off."

"This shit's better music than we're playing. Man, I never realized how pedestrian pop songs were."

"Pedestrian? What the hell kind a word is that? Pedestrian?"

"Guys," Blain will say, lifting the shoulder strap of his lead guitar over his head and setting the instrument down across the amplifier. "Let's take a break. I gotta piss, anyway. You want something from the kitchen? My mom made chicken last night. How about a snack, huh, guys? Come on in and let's finish off that chicken."

Before Ely thinks they're ready, the dance will come over the rise and make them put up or shut up, there and then. And what they will discover is that Blain, usually soft spoken during rehearsal, not only knows the words to every song, but can sing them while fondling the microphone with invisible hands, his own busy on lead guitar, re-styling even a dance ditty into soft porn for the underclass girls. His solos will be musically sound, but all the more captivating because he loves to have people love him and performing will become his courting ritual. His cropped hair and boyishly charming eyes an album cover clamoring for print; his unbridled hips and willful smile the gossip of mothers, the rumors of daughters.

Oh, they will ride that night out like a cowboy straddling a cruise missile, eight seconds not enough for the euphoria to radiate to every stitch of their midnight blue Wranglers jeans. A rumbling pickup ride down toward the ridge later, bottled beer will be shaken up and sprayed over their heads as if they had brought home the Lombardi Trophy, Winston Cup, and Holy Grail all at once. And to the shouts for an encore, they will only be able to grin an indefatigable grin, shrug, and try to holler over the orgasmic mob's cadence, "Our instruments're back at the school!"

"We are gettin' the hell outta this town!" Blain will beam as the three of them find it hard to bear down and practice, sitting around his garage the Monday after the dance, still aglow in their exaltation. "Damn! I never really dreamed we'd get a chance like this."

"What chance? All we've got is a couple dozen covers. We gotta start writing something of our own. Something with our name on it."

"Hang on," Ely will say to Dusty's fervor, and someday look back and wonder if that weren't the first place it all turned sour. "Write our own music? We've been writing music everyday for the past coupla years, and we haven't made a single complete song yet."

"No, we've just been playing around, learning. But if we set down and get to it—"

"What are you talking about? We only played the high school dance. That's it. There wasn't no agents from Nashville thrustin' their cards in my face. No, we got that gig by nailing those covers, and that's what we gotta keep on doin' now. We gotta get every new hit record before anyone knows it's a hit and learn the songs before people even know they wanna hear 'em, and then we'll get gigs from here to Tucson."

"There's only Phoenix between here and Tucson," Dusty will say as anti-climatic punctuation.

" Well, there's Prescott," Blain will add for the record, his voice trailing off.

"How do you think Dwayne Tucker and his boys got on the road?" Ely will say to make his point.

But Dusty will have none of that. "And look where Dwayne Tucker still is: auditioning for high school dances in cow piss towns like this. The world's a whole lot bigger than the Colorado Plateau, Ely. You see all them kids on MTV. They didn't hang around playin' the oldies waitin' for some big break. They went out and grabbed the bull by the balls."

Ely will see that there will be no detour. It will be no use to say that they aren't punk rockers and that country fans like their music seasoned from life, not spiked with angst. He will see it clearly: they will have to drive through that rough patch. But not before its time.

"All right," he will say, "you write what you want, and when you have something decent, we'll throw it around and see what it turns into. All right? But in the meantime we can't just put down our instruments and try to be cowboy poets. We still have to practice."

And practice they will. Brooks and Dunn, Randy Travis, Alabama, Sawyer Brown, and too many upstart groups barely older than these three boys to keep track of. Whoever ever had a hit or looks like they will, these boys who never want to see sawdust in the cuffs of their shirts or safety glasses hanging from the sun visor of their trucks will learn it all and play it well. But Ely will know that this is a prison escape only, and that once they have put the confines of this town safely behind them that there will be nothing to keep them together. So when he hears Dusty pull a change-up on the tempo of a two-step classic, he won't say anything, because fighting won't get them anywhere, and he wants to get anywhere but here.

He will understand that Dusty's vague concept of a destination is not the same as his own daydream of not even glancing at the sight of Cliffside receding in the rear view mirror for the very last time. He will understand how Dusty yearns to arrive, while he dreads capture and would not mind being perpetually presented with highway horizons that he is never able to pursue to their ends.

"We've got an audition," Blain will announce once they've gathered in his garage for practice one May afternoon. "The county fair!"

"We got it?" Ely will ask in elation.

"It's just an audition."

"It's just a county fair," Dusty will mutter, heard by all.

"County fair's the biggest venue in these parts," Blain will say flatly, taking no one's side. "So let's get our set together, because our audition is less than two weeks away. They're taking on lots of bands, but the time slots are what's important. If we get in the evening time slot, that's prime time. A drinking crowd."

"And that means the stand-by's. We gotta be ready for that. Most of the crowd'll be older," Ely will suggest, hoping Dusty can not argue for once.

"We get this and we play it well, and we'll have a foot in the door on the bar circuit. There's already people talkin' about us, my Dad says. I know this ain't the big record deal, Dusty, but it's a step in that direction," Blain will say.

"Hey, what are you looking at me for? Let's get started," Dusty will say.

They will come together again like they did before at the high school audition, clutching not only an evening slot, but the nine-to-midnight slot, on the main stage, beating out Dwayne Tucker's boys and relegating them to the six-to-nine slot. Before their set that first night of the three day fair, they'll bump into Dwayne, coming down off his set, and, being rushed, they'll make a quick promise to have a beer during their break. So when it's almost a quarter to eleven, and their second break is coming up, all three of them will start getting nervous and Blain will even skip a whole line of lyrics, bringing a few harmless but annoyed heckles from the crowd of eased-up cowboy shirts.

Dwayne Tucker will be standing alone in a fresh outfit next to the bleachers, arms folded, his cowboy hat brim low, but face held up enough that they can recognize him. He'll clap politely, not enthusiastically, at the end of the set, and while the boys are putting their instruments down, he'll wave a waitress his way and secure a table, order four beers. The boys will be sweaty, especially Dusty, who doesn't move around as much as Blain, but who sweats more all the same. Blain will be scanning the tables and bleachers beyond them for the couple of girls who were flirting with him earlier, though he knows they're just high school juniors, and their mommas probably called them home by now.

"Good set, boys," Dwayne will say. "Gave me a few ideas."

"Thanks," Ely will say. "You guys were good, too."

"Don't kid a kidder, boy. We're gettin' old. We gotta pick up on that new sound like you boys done. Past few years we've been playin' so much, darn near every night—thanks, Hon. Why don't you put that on my tab for now, all right? And tell ol' Red I said Hey—we been playin' so much we ain't had time to work much new material into the act, anyway not the flashy stuff the kiddies like. You boys are good at it, though." He will pause to sip deeply from the translucent plastic cup of beer, leaving the boys to their collective anxiety at why Dwayne Tucker, two of whose recent gigs they have usurped, wants to talk to them, and whether the rest of his boys are waiting in the parking area with tire irons. "Yeah. So here's what I wanna do for you. I wanna show you the ropes, introduce you to a few people, and set you on your way to fame and fortune."

The boys, sipping cautiously the alcohol they wouldn't have been served in any normal circumstance, won't know what to think of this, but Blain will venture a guess. "You wanna be our manager?"

Hearing that, Tucker will guffaw, his head tilted back under the strings of lights and colorful plastic triangles like those from a used car lot radiating overhead from the stage to the bleachers. Keeping a broad grin on his face he will somehow look into the eyes of all three of them at once and say, "No, I don't care to be your manager. I just wanna help you boys get on to bigger and better things. For two reasons: first, because you're good enough to do it; and second, because I'm tired a you eatin' my steak already."

And that's how things will get rolling. Dwayne will line up auditions for them at some of the bars he plays in, and even a few he hasn't been scheduled in for awhile. The fact that they're underage will be side-stepped by any number of technicalities, and they'll trek northern Arizona like seasoned hobos. They'll make regular appearances in Prescott, Payson, and Flagstaff—where the Museum Club will shit bricks they didn't want them and they end up headlining a few nights a week all summer over in downtown, where mostly punk and jazz are played—and spend a few nights in Winslow, Show Low, and the like.

"But it's still just small towns," Dusty will say in their van on the way from a Friday night in Prescott to a motel and Saturday night set in Flagstaff. "Just bigger small towns. We're just making enough money for gas, motels, and food. We've gotta seriously think about turning it up a notch. Playing our own stuff, you know."

"Dusty, we're still in high school. After graduation, we'll be free to just keep drivin'. Dwayne and the boys head down to Austin, Texas and spend a whole week playin' a different club every night there. And we'll get more money. We could be gettin' more money now, but I'd rather get the gigs. This time next year, we'll be household names across the whole state, and then what? Wyoming? Texas?"

"Look, we can play some of your stuff, if it's ready," Ely will add to Blain's comments. "I mean, if it fits with our audiences, of course."

Dusty will sit quietly for a moment. "I haven't gotten anything solid written yet. We've been too busy on the road, and I'm still trying to graduate, so I'm doing as much reading as I can keep my eyes open for."

"All right. Me too. Look, I don't wanna spend my whole life on the road like this," Ely will say, knowing that at some level it is a lie. "But we're just breakin' in right now. Learnin' the business. Just be patient."

Winter on the Colorado Plateau will be marked by the flocking of California snowbirds to the ski slopes north of Flagstaff, and the southern migration of wealthy retirees to the golf courses of Sedona. Insisting they concentrate on school, the boys' parents will impose a hibernatic home life, devastating no one, because all will be exhausted and the break will do them good. Still, there will be the sensation of a doomed rocket spiraling into a deteriorating orbit, pulled back to where it launched from without ever having arrived at where it intended, perhaps not even having reached escape velocity.

But the sudden eruption of the rumor about Blain will threaten their whole mission. Blain and all the women at shows they won't mind, but this they will not be able to turn away from.

"Blain, why didn't you tell us anything? Is she really pregnant? Is it yours?"

"Ely, I don't know, man. She said… I don't know. Look, we dated a little when I was a sophomore, and we got together one night after we played at the Outpost. She and a friend drove up to watch. Anyway, I don't know."

"Dammit, Blain, not yet. You wanna mess everything up after we make it, I don't care. But we gotta make it first, man."

"Dusty's right. This is us, Blain. The three of us. We're doin' this together, and can't none of us ruin it for the other two. Not me, not any of us. Now, if she *is* pregnant… Oh, man, I hope it ain't true."

So they will sweat out a few weeks until Sharon, the girl, finally has her period, and tells Blain she thought she was pregnant, though no one believes for a minute that she hadn't fabricated the whole thing.

Graduation will be an anti-climatic interruption in the accelerating late spring resurgence of rambling live music and the obligations it brings. The boys will barely be able to practice for all the road time, gigs, and debt to sleep with ever-accruing interest. Then, on an over-niter in the valley, in a college club within sight of the Sun Devil's stadium, where middle-of-the-road rock is the house flavor, the boys will have a late dinner with the owner.

" Wish you boys would've had a bigger crowd to play to tonight, but Thursday through Saturday is when the kids flock in here, and they prefer rock, you know."

Miles Roy, the owner, will have treated them to the rib-eye, the most expensive item on the menu, an act which Blain appreciated as if it were a favor long overdue. Roy will wear a tie to compliment his long-sleeved shirt, which openly announces his non-Arizona origins. "What kind a fool wears a tie in Tempe?" will be Ely's after-dinner appraisal back in the confines of the van, preceded by, "His parents named him backwards." But that won't be the way Dusty and Blain see it. If a man has clubs in five different cities, he can dress how he wants and have "Daffy Duck" printed on his business cards.

During the dinner, Roy will continue, "These kids don't appreciate a good down-home sound. I've got two clubs in Kansas City, two in Nashville, and I'm part-owner of some of the best live clubs in Austin and New Orleans. Those are music cities, boys. Folks who come to hear you play know what they're hearing. My clubs have introduced big names before they were big, and welcomed them back to promote their hit records. We've even hosted some live national broadcasts. God knows why I branched into Arizona. But, anyway, let's get down to business. I don't want to see you playing sad venues like this on Monday nights. You've got too much talent for that. See, I can't play a note, but I've got an ear. So, if you're up to it, I'd like to offer you a little time in Kansas City, to start. We can see how the crowd takes to you there, and if all goes well, I can get you on a rotation of my clubs, and maybe introduce you to some other owners, eventually."

Ely will listen, chewing his steak slowly, waiting for the other shoe to drop. But when it doesn't, he will probe. "I don't mean to be rude, but what's in it for you? You're just gonna put us in your clubs and help launch our career… all for nothing?"

"No, son. I will get something out of it. If I have the best new talent playing my clubs, I have the best clubs. You'd be amazed at how much money comes in when you have a headliner. But," Roy will say, down shifting, "you boys aren't headliners, yet. Make no mistake: it's up to you. I think you've got what it takes, and you can go as far as you want. But I have seen better acts than you fall apart. I'm taking a little risk, putting you on my stage, I know. If you bomb in my club, that's going to cost me for weeks, or even months, until folks trust my taste in music again. Maybe what I've heard about you and what I saw tonight was all there is to you. Even worse, maybe it was a brilliant moment for a mundane band. But I don't think so, and I'm willing to bet on it. Are you? Because I'm not giving you an annual contract. I'm not saying I'm going to hook you up with an agent or a producer. I'm saying that you are invited to come to my clubs and give it your best shot. I plan to work you one weekend in each club, and do it over again if it goes well. But, like I said, that might just be the beginning."

Blain's father will be thrilled by the news; both Dusty and Ely's dads will wonder what's so bad about their life in their town that their sons don't like the taste of it. All of their mothers will fluctuate between the worry and envy that an adolescent's freedom triggers.

Kansas City. Before the first two weeks are up, Roy will sit them down to talk about taking their act to his other clubs. During that lunch, he will say, "And don't be afraid to work some of your own stuff into the act. If you're ever going to snag a recording deal, it'll be from your own songs."

That will be enough to throw the whole thing out of balance. Ely won't have squat to say to stop Dusty from whipping it up with his odd beats. Here they'll be, half way to where they think they're going—or away from where they're leaving—but not yet a safe enough distance from the undertow of home, and Dusty will be risking it all because he wants to make ripples in the music world.

"I know we gotta write our own stuff," Ely will plead, "but I just think we should stick to a standard format. We know what we're good at, so let's stick with it. It got us this far."

"How far? To a motel room shared three ways and a twelve year-old van that could leave us stranded along any given highway? We haven't made it anywhere at all. We're on the way, all right, but we still just got one foot stuck in the door. The only way we're gonna break all the way free is to make a name for ourselves. And cover bands don't do that."

"I said we don't have to do just covers. We can write some stuff, but..."

"But make it sound just like the stuff we're already playing, right? Don't you think they'll see through that?"

Sitting on the corner at the foot of the bed, watching them so close at the tiny round table, growing so frustrated with one another, Blain will not worry that it might escalate, as he will have seen this many times before.

Knowing all the arguments have been made in the past, and that Dusty has grown adept at fending them all off, Ely will reach for his trump card. "Well, I'm not sure what it is you want, then. But we're a country band, Dusty, not a jazz quartet."

"What are you talking about?" Dusty will say, genuinely confused.

"You've been spending every night off roaming around to jazz clubs. I know. And that crap you've been pullin' out in practice, that's not country, either: that's jazz."

"So what? If it fits in a country song, maybe that's the ticket we've been looking for."

"Jazz and country? What country band you know with a saxophone and trumpet?"

"None. Not a one. Not a single, stinking one. But you know what? That doesn't mean it won't work out. That just means no one else has had the guts to try it."

"And you're gonna be the one, huh?"

"Let me tell you this, Ely: I'll play these covers to get out of Cliffside. But if I become famous, it won't be as a hack."

As they make the rounds of Roy's clubs, Blain will pick up a habit of long-distance phone calls home, but not to his family. By the time they get done in Nashville, each of the boys will have his own motel room, so no one will hear Blain's sweet talk; no one will hear the friction between Dusty and Ely like a meteor burning up so high in the atmosphere.

And then Austin. The smell of burning fingertips sanding themselves down across the cords of a lead guitar. A nightlife sauntering along to the steady, soothing beat of a bass. With thunder not from a storm, but raising into the sky from rebellious percussionists. Austin will be their chance. Austin will be their dream.

The name they all know from the credits in album jackets, now embossed in gold flake on a black business card, extended to each of the three, their heads still dizzy from the sweaty, driven set just played. Smiles exploding wide, slugs on the upper arm, arms clasped around shoulders, and Blain nearly crying with joy as he doubles over, faint from exhaustion and exhilaration, then snaps back up so far he arcs his back and howls over the heads of the crowd around them. The crowd with no idea how close they'll make it to actually making it.

But then Dusty will cut the celebration short by politely saying, "Well, we'll talk about it."

Noticeably ruffled by what must be the first time any brash young country band had ever not shaken on a deal on the spot, the producer will say, "Boys, if you don't call my number before I change my mind, it'll likely be the biggest mistake you're ever privileged enough to make."

"You can't be serious! Are you out of your mind?" Ely will bellow, nearly as upset at Blain for not being outraged as he is at Dusty for refusing to sign the contract. "This is a package deal. They want us. Us! This is what we've been doing all this for. You're the one who wanted a contract, man! What the—how can you just walk away from it—from us—now?"

"Look, this has been building for a while now. Don't act like it's a big surprise."

"Well, it is a surprise, Dusty. It's a big kick-in-the-crotch surprise!" Ely will try to calm himself, try to make his words sound inviting, not threatening. But the motel room like a cave seen through a fish-eye lens and his head pounding from the pressure of hot blood hassle his self-control. "A record label wants us to sign, and you have some artistic conflict? To hell with your artistic conflict. Sign the contract, Dusty!"

But Dusty will simply say, matter-of-factly, "This isn't what I want to do any more, Ely."

"This isn't what we'll be doing! We won't be scraping dimes together for gas no more. We'll be in a studio, and then on a tour. A real tour with our names on a bus, man!"

"That's not what I mean. It's this… us… the way we… " and then Dusty will find his words: "There's no harmony left between us."

Begging, promising, angry, desperate phone calls over the next few days will be of no use. Dusty's mind will not be changed.

Faced with the prospect of filling Dusty's shoes, the producer will explain that he might as well just look for a whole new band, because the chances of finding the right drummer with the right magic for that threesome is slim to none. "Unique flavors can't be whipped up that way," he will say. And, with that, the world tumbles out of orbit.

You could find yourself suddenly cresting thirty, looking back and looking in front, and finding that only the young have dreams, and yours have been usurped by anxieties. What if you never have another chance like that?

You will find that of these three boys, all of them had the hunger to get out of that tiny hometown, but none of them had the appetite to be a star. The big city and fame meant nothing to any of them, after all. Blain sold the van to Ely for a few uncollected favors and a handful of bills, took a Greyhound home and married, then divorced, then remarried Sharon, that same girl who had caused ripples early on. Blain loved the spotlight, but he never wanted to be more than a big fish in a little pond. The national tour, the bright lights, were just to have a story to tell, braggin' rights: just to add a magnitude more of brightness to his winning smile. All his dreams came true the moment the recording contract was offered, and he didn't have time to imagine new ones before it became apparent there was no use in daydreaming, so he will always feel that he went out on top. He plays with a new band he got together, making the rounds on summer evenings, holding down a day job, too.

Dusty. Well, Dusty pretty much made good on his threats to succeed by doing what he wanted. Not two years went by before his name started appearing in the liner notes of one jazz release after another. His is a name you hear a lot if you're in the business, but fans only notice if they read the "special thanks to" lines of CD jackets. He's got a good reputation behind him now, and is riding it like the wind.

Ely? Ely is a hard story for me to tell. His has been a bitter pill, caught in his throat these past several years. Call him a studio musician, because at least he has found steady work at that, his meticulous nature being appreciated by many a rising star. He's formed a few bands over the years, but nothing with any spice. Just played the same old haunts. And he may just have been happy enough doing this, too, if only he had never had and missed a chance to be more. In the last few years, he's begun to see where Dusty may have been right. But he won't chastise himself about that, right now. See, there's no moral to this fable until you decide how it ends, and this one will keep humming along.

Thunder on a Clear Day

For a moment, the sky showers thunder and I can't hear him breathing. No heartbeat. Only the slight swelling of his chest, which lifts the weight of my reposing head, lets me know he is still here, alive, with me. The sky above is clear. Mechanical thunder from a jet, which I see miles distant from its sound, lows through these skies often. Supersonic: like a teenage summer love affair. Then the beating resumes. Distant, but not like the jet. More muffled, as if hidden beneath avalanches of barriers, trying to let someone know it is there. The beating is quick, almost frantic. It's always like that, even when he sleeps—especially when he sleeps. Becoming desperate in dreams, anxious in nightmares, I don't know. Maybe when he sleeps his heart senses that somewhere in that inconceivable pile of barricades there is a weakness, a path, and it clamors all the more vigorously for freedom.

Do I only imagine that his hair, his skin, still exude that faint odor of burnt motor oil, even on his day off? Waiting for him to wake, I reach over lazily and put the Tupperware lid back on the container of potato salad. So odd, that salad. Though I've always detested celery in my otherwise smooth potato salad—the way my mother always made it—as I made that batch I found myself slicing up the celery. Even as I was slicing it I thought that I didn't really want it in my salad, but I tipped the cutting board over the mixing bowl and pushed it in with the flat side of the knife, all the same.

The residue of the watermelon like Velcro between my fingers annoys me steadily, but I can't reach the cooler to dip my fingers in the melt-water. So I just close my eyes against the steady sun and wrap my arm toward his head, toward the hair I would run my fingers through, if they were not so sticky—if I didn't fear waking him.

Shuddering abruptly, he awakes, forcing me sit up suddenly. It's nearly three in the afternoon on another Sunday, and although I am not working, I do not feel relaxed. I love his company, I guess, but sometimes I resent not being able to just be alone with me. He sits up, stretches a little, cracks his neck (I hate that sound), then reaches into the cooler for a beer. The can makes that crisp breaking sound when he opens it. He puts the can to his lips for a second, then pulls it away with a look of disgust and spits yellow liquid onto the grass, hitting the blanket we're on, too. "Warm!" he says, not yet to me, but to the surrounding animals, people, and trees which certainly have been awaiting his report. He tilts the can and impatiently pours the beer into the grass, watching with a scourging glare, as if he were punishing peasants for insolence. "Let's go get something cold to drink," he says, for the first time acknowledging my presence, though his eyes still haven't met mine. He gets up and heads to the car. Shaking off the grass and bugs and crumbs with a few quick snaps, I haphazardly bundle up the blanket, grab the cooler, and catch up with him. He's always like this when he wakes up.

He has more than one "something cold to drink." It is around seven and he's not himself again. Or maybe this is his true self, and the sober guy is an alias. Anyway, the beer has gotten to him, so we end up at my place. With the curtains drawn, it's somewhat dark inside, so the blinking red eye on the answering machine is prominent. As he heads through the bedroom toward the bathroom I set the cooler just inside the kitchen doorway, with the blanket on top, then kneel beside the telephone table and press the "Play" button on the machine. The first is just a wrong number, so I fast forward through the annoying tone. As soon as the second starts, even before I hear the voice, I hear the same wetting of lips which I always hear at the beginning of her messages. So my finger skims across to the "Stop" button. Mother. I don't need this now.

He's got sleep on his mind, but the last time his mind made a decision for him was before puberty. He seems to think he has to give me the lay-of-my-life every time we're alone. His front of super-confidence is just a coating to waterproof his weaknesses, I know. There I go again, pretending I can guess his psyche. Might as well guess people's weight and age while I'm at it, and at least I could charge a buck for the novelty.

So in his stupor he gets his pants off, but leaves his shirt and socks on, and fucks me with his eyes open only enough to know it's still light out. I can't say it's my favorite part of spending time with him, but there's no sense in trying to stop him. That'd only spark an argument about whether or not I like having sex with him, which I usually do. Men are so fragile.

Before he passes out in sweaty exhaustion and relief, he moans something about a perfect weekend. Maybe for him. Personally, I could still use that dose of peace that's been on back-order. I swing my legs over and get out of bed, covering him to the waist with the sheet. How is it that he can't get himself undressed, but all of my clothes are flung to the remote corners of the room? I take a white button-down from its hanger in the open closet and I fasten the bottom two buttons as I pick up my panties with the toe of one foot.

His mysteries seem so near the surface when he sleeps. His eyes become gentle, forsaking the piercing glare always found there when he's awake. His brow relaxes, and everything seems calm, inviting, tender… vulnerable. I feel I could reach in and encounter that beating something that so desperately wants out. Or extract one by one those blockades, barriers, and battlements that permeate him. But I know better. I only suppose I know what I'd find, but can't be certain. It's only my fantasy. He's not mine to manipulate, anyway. Just a man. Just a good time. Just someone who will leave, not because of me, he'll say (although I know better), but "because of his job." Someone who wants to be a lover, but not in love. Who wants to know my everything, but does not know the meaning of "share." Who wants to know my everything not because he cares, but because he supposes that I want to tell him, and he wishes to humor my desires as long as possible. Without remembering my favorite flavor of ice-cream, or my home town, or why exactly I dropped out of college. Without caring who the last man was, or when I plan to settle down, or why I cry when that certain song is played. But asks me all the same, as if I had some need to expose my soul to him before sleeping with him. As if I needed to feel pain before pleasure, which, if it ever is pleasure, is only fleeting, soon to be replaced by the longing that it truly is: no more than a contribution to the scar tissue on my heart. Confusing me into thinking that he's sincere, that he's the first one who won't leave. But leaving me with a lump in my throat some morning until he's driven out of sight and I can cry like I need to. That's what I really need to do: cry. Cry for all the bridges I've burned, always on accident, so young in my life, and the mistakes I feel can never be erased. Cry because he's just a man, but he seems so childlike, and I want to help him, hold him more than anything else, and comfort him and tell him it's all right, but I know I can't. Because he's just a man.

I pull the door until it starts to get tight in the jam, then leave it ajar that much so the noise of shutting it completely doesn't bother him. If I wake him, there goes my quiet time alone. Stiff, once-upon-a-time shag carpet now resists my bare feet more like a cross-stitch piece which weathered a hurricane. Flat, matted patches here and there among the overgrowth of wild yarn. Could it ever have been plush, or anything less than abrasive? Rentals. Layers of other people's paint; cheap carpet the landlord found at a garage sale fifteen years ago; windows that don't open right or close securely because of those generations of paint; smudges on the plastic frames around the light switches and outlet plates—some of which are white and some beige; dust along the top of the baseboards, which are typically the same color as the walls—often white—like they were being weather-proofed or preserved together, and which further foreground the dust because it's the only seam along the smooth scar of accumulated paint from floor to rain-leak-stained ceiling.

I don't risk turning on the TV and waking him, but just put in a CD and play it low. The answering machine's red numeral and blinking eye plead for my attention as I pass, panties still in-hand, to the kitchen. Sorry, but you just want to ruin my peace. No matter how harmoniously I strive to accompany Annie Lennox, anyone within earshot can only hear a timid woman with bare feet flat against the unaccoustic grit of Linoleum in a kitchen with cupboard hardware too rickety to pose as a sound booth. As the water heats up in the microwave, I put on my panties and sit at the table, legs drawn up from the cool floor. Tilting my head back, I capture the proper angle and see in the rain-stain over my table the scene of a horse galloping up a cloud of dust. When the microwave bell rings, I wish I'd stopped it prematurely, just so as not to risk waking him. He'll be asleep most of the evening, and then won't able to sleep tonight, but that'll be his own fault. He'll whine about being too tired for work in the morning, but I'll have slept right through the old war movie he'll find on some cable channel, and I'll go to work fifteen minutes early and won't have to hear about it.

Walking tenderly on the brown and gold pine needle carpet's worn path back into the living room, I smoothly stir the spinning island of cocoa under the water's surface. I could drink hot-cocoa on an Indonesian beach in August. It's relaxation in a mug, for me. But a hot mug. So I set it on the glass-topped table between the rocker and the rattan catalog-ordered couch that I hate. It looked so cozy—and was an affordable way to help fill up the living room—but when you sit in it, you're cast back so you can hardly get out of its cup-shaped cushion. You have to really be planning on staying there awhile to make it worth the effort of getting back up. The dully-dust-coated magazine covers glance at me from their plastic cubicles—those milk-crate style, stackable ones—but fail to grab my attention.

Pulling the curtains open, I see the breeze has picked up and is buffeting the high wildflowers across the road. The walls pale to a shadow of white as the sun falls behind a cloud. Even when the sun reappears, the room stays somewhat dim because the sun is over the trees now. The day is winding down. Through the sheers I watch the neighbor's cat hop up on my car's hood to sunbathe. If I had clothes on, I might open the door and scare it away. Then a couple walks by on the sidewalk, looks toward the house, and I wonder if the man, whose glance lingers, can see my breasts from there. Still, I don't button up the shirt. Let them look. What would you say to that, Mother? That's why you called, right? To remind me to straighten out my life? Well maybe someone should remind you that it's my life.

Without purpose, I ease into the rocker. The sheepskin cover is matted on the seat, but still softer than the carpet, and warmer than the sleeping air around me. The kitchen clock's tapping both defines and overpowers the taciturn ambiance between songs. Lackluster. That framed print has got to go the next time I move. I'm sure I thought it looked fine before, but now its drabness (in fact, it's even cornily drab, like a parody of dullness) dominates the wall, which would be more interesting with only the nail's own shadow hanging in lieu of the picture.

Jesus, it's exhausting trying not to look at that damned little red light. Come, come, come, come, come, come, come, its patient mantra repeats like blown kisses. No, no, no, no, no, I think, picking up the cocoa, giving it a last swirl and hugging it near my neck to feel its warmth.

On top of the stacked milk-crate shelves lies a letter, collecting dust since Thursday. If I don't read it another will come, and when I don't read that one, either, Mom will call to see if I received them. She'll give me the same lecture over the phone as in the letter. So I know that reading it and writing back would be the easiest way, but maybe if I ignore it long enough the words will become bored and entertain themselves by re-arranging into sentiments which wouldn't offend or agitate me. They'd talk about the weather, and the Senate race, and the new sit-com on Tuesdays. But nothing about me. No pointed, wiggling fingers, cataloging whatever might be wrong with my life and the way I live it. Let's face it: such neutral words will not likely come from her pen. Not until I've been canonized will the words be benign. In the meantime, all is malicious.

She doesn't even know about him. But she's seen them come and go and can guess. But I'm twenty-six years old, dammit, and I have a right to have sex. What would you say to that, Mother? Would you lecture me on the benefits of chastity?

No. I suppose not. That's not your style.

So what? Should I write you back? That'd be easier than calling you. But calling would get it over with sooner. I could just pick up the phone right now, dial you up and say, "Hey, Mom, what's your problem? Why do you think there's something wrong with my life? Because I don't go to church anymore? Because I dropped out of college? Because I'm having sex? Come on. What disappoints you the most about my life?"

And what would she say? Would she critique every mistake I've made over the last few years? No, she'd be reserved. "Honey," she might say, "we all make decisions we regret."

"But they were my decisions," I'd say. "It's none of your business. Why do you think I'm not happy? I have a nice place here." She'd never know it's only half true: she's never been to visit. "I have a good job at the trucking company. Not every college drop-out—or graduate, for that matter—becomes the assistant director of public relations for a national trucking company in only two and a half years."

And she'd say… well, she wouldn't cut me down. She never tried to cut me down. She'd say something like, "I know that, Dear. I've been hoping for the opportunity to tell you how well you've done."

Then I'd want to tell her she could have just called anytime, but she knows as well as I do that it's me who won't return her calls. So I'll drop that one.

"Is it college, then? Are you disappointed that I dropped out? Is that it? Well it wasn't a total waste, you know. I can go back anytime I want to and finish. I've been thinking about that a lot lately. I might take some night classes," I'd say.

Still, she'd be understanding. "That sounds like a good opportunity for you, Dear," she might say.

"So," I'd say, "are you upset about my personal life? I know you wish I'd get married, but I'm just not ready. So maybe the guys I date aren't husband material, but someday the right kind of guy will come along. But why can't you accept that? Is it the church? Is it all that chastity bull that the Bible goes on about? Well, that's *your* god talking, Mother."

"*My* god?" she'd clarify, and I'd know I had her. "Honey, God is the same. For all eternity. He doesn't just go through phases like us."

And I'd be ready for her. "That's not true," I'd say, calmly. I'd want to frustrate and flabbergast her with this one. "God's changing all the time. A few hundred years ago, women couldn't be ministers, but now they can be."

"Honey," she'd say, too patiently for me to believe she was just trying to keep her temper—so much it would make me want to chew the phone cord in half, "that's not God changing. That's people's minds. Yes, women can be ordained now, but skirt lengths have also changed in my lifetime. And even though our society has, for the most part, evolved into acceptance of these new ideas, that doesn't mean anything in relation to the immutability of God. Next year skirt lengths will probably change again. And the death sentence and abortion and drugs and the purpose of education will be hotly debated until after I die, too. But even if everyone suddenly agrees and the debate ends, it doesn't mean the solution was right or wrong—

not on any universal level. It just means we've reached consensus. And consensus is not Truth: it's merely justification."

And then I'd hang up. In my mind, at least. She always has to be right. And using words like "immutable." She'd change this into a religious discussion when it's really just about me living my life.

Drinking the cooling, last thick bit of cocoa, I take the mug to the kitchen and place it gingerly in the sink. As I return to the rocker, I pick up the phone and pull the slack cord from around behind the table, resting the phone in my lap, then closing my eyes to the music. One of those planes goes over and until the jet is ten miles away the only sound is the bombardment of waves of nothing against the ground—like intentions tumbling and smashing from hopeless heights. I've missed part of my favorite song, but it doesn't matter: I have the feeling I'll be sitting here long enough to hear it come around again. I don't want to be in there, with him. Not now. I don't want to go anywhere, do anything. Just sit and think about nothing, not even memories, and let things fall into place invisibly while I'm totally unawares. It takes doing that every now and then to keep going.

The sounds of him getting up, then a groan as he goes to the bathroom without shutting the door because he never shuts the door. I crane my neck and see him emerge from the bathroom in only his t-shirt now, pausing long enough to put some underwear on and open the window for the cool breeze before going back to bed. He'll be out all night.

Of course she'll call back. Leaving a message on a machine wouldn't satisfy her, and it doesn't tell her what I'm thinking.

So go ahead and ring. I have some wisdom for you, too, Mom. You see, no one has what they want now. You have to be patient, because good things come to those who wait.

Cerberus on the Mogollon Rim

"Shouldn't you be out reporting the news, Bradford?" Jake Schepper said, his eyes barely skimming my face as he scanned the room, the door closing too heavily under its own power behind him.

"Show me where to find some, and I'll report it," I said.

I sat facing the door, under the arch of letters which spelled out Stump's Diner backwards and inside-out, compared to the image on the street, on the wide front window. Jake took his cowboy hat off, exposing two white peaks above his red brow, and flanks of brittle-looking, graying hair overgrowing the ears, crimped in an even line by the weight of the hat. A rancher removes his hat with the uncomfortable security of a man undressing in a doctor's office, mutual evasion of eye-contact providing a refutation of the act. It's a by-law of the range that you don't make fun of a man's hair as long as he covers it up again within a few seconds. He held the crown of the hat just before his chin and blew on it with care, as if handling an antique, evicting a small plume of dust.

"Get dusty from sittin' on a fence rail?" Clyde Parsons asked, seeing as Schepper had once again donned his hat.

"Could get dusty riding in a truck with the windows up in this wind," Schepper said.

"Which way's it blowin' now?" Bob Fletcher asked. Bob and Clyde were seated across from each other, staggered by one seat, at a long cafeteria style table.

"'Round," Schepper answered. He grabbed a chair like a dog by the scruff of the neck, yanked it a full yard from the table and reclined there as if he had intended to occupy the aisle until Janet took his order, then scooted forward as she turned toward the kitchen.

"Hey, Bradford, what's the weather forecast today?" Parsons said. It was just the four of us, and Janet and Helen in the kitchen, so there was no need to even raise his voice.

"Couldn't tell you," I said. "Didn't you listen to the radio?"

"Why listen to the radio when we have our own local newspaper editor right here every morning?"

"Now, have you ever seen a weather report in the *Courier*? We only publish twice a week, gentlemen. Would you really want me to guess at the weather that far out? Anyway, I come here to get the news from you, not give it out."

Bob went to the trouble of holding his hand beside his mouth like a privacy fence as he made an aside to Clyde, which meant it must have been an unusually rude comment for him to not want me to hear. Clyde laughed politely. His loyalties are first to fellow ranchers, after all.

"Tell you one thing," Helen called from through the horizontal opening to the kitchen where finished orders were placed. "We need rain."

Quote of the day material, that. Through the front window the tops of cottonwoods on the street behind the post office could be seen tussling with a swirling foe. People were just then waking up to find that persistent wind still on the rampage like a stray dog strewing garbage across their lawns for the umpteenth day in a row. But the wind was just the most concrete entity they could blame for the anxiety which pervaded more moments of each new day as the dry spell—which was an absence, not a presence, and so could not be held accountable as the wind could be—trudged forward, defying all projections of when it might break.

"You sec that?" Bob said. I turned to look, but they were all looking at the window. "We got ourselves a tourist. Red Chevy. Just went by."

"Hope they ain't come up for the campin'. That's what started that doozie up there in Flagstaff. Some camper from the valley decided to start a fire."

"Heard they lost a thousand acres to that one."

"Yep. Wind got hold of it and took it right up the side of Mt. Elden."

"Thousand acres! That right, Bradford?"

"A thousand and forty is what we printed," I answered. I was proud to have called the Forest Service and gotten my own information instead of mining it out of stories on the CNN website like I often had to do for facts and figures.

I looked back out the window. Behind the post office, beyond those cottonwoods, you could point to where the smoke had hung, smeared and hazy in the distance, until just a few days ago. Then you might turn yourself around slowly, one inch at a time, scan the horizon close and far, peering to discern the wisp of a shadow above the next wildfire.

Where is there to go in this town when you gotta be alone? When you get a letter like this, not even handed to you, and you gotta be alone?

Kick me outta this forest? I don't think so! Hell, I've been rompin' around these hills all my life. Those locked gates are for the damned hippies outta Sedona, come up here and smoke their pot and dance around naked. Yeah, keep them out before they burn the whole place down around themselves. Ought to know better than to play with matches in someone else's house, anyways. But I know the fence only stretches wide enough to reach the first trees on either side of the road, and that ain't gonna stop me. So I just shift into four-high and hump it around the fence. I know the spare key's under the mat, if you know what I mean.

If you can't trust a Hot-Shot in the forest, who can you trust? And I'm gonna be a Hot-Shot, too. Just one more year a high school, and I'll be training to be the best a the best. Don't want no one from town to see me tonight, though, 'cause them look-out boys can be real serious times like this. So I turn my lights out while I drive over the rise, down into the ravine, around the mountain. Know these roads like my own backyard. Coulda done it with my eyes closed.

Drop the tailgate down, hop up and lay back in the bed, my lower legs dangling. Her note—she couldn't say it to my face, or even over the phone—held by both hands across my chest. The pines howl and swish. This damn wind. I sit up and reach for the quarter bottle of Jack I swiped from Dad's truck. He'll just think one a his buddies went home with it in their cab. Anyways, he's got three or four more opened bottles here and there all around the house.

Hope she calls. Hope she calls because she feels miserable about layin' it on me this way, and my folks'll say I'm out on a date, because that's what I told 'em, and she'll wonder who I found so fast, and they'll say they don't know, and she'll be the one sittin' at home knowin' there's questions to be asked and no one to answer 'em for her.

First to arrive, last to leave, Fletcher and Parsons lingered in front of the diner before heading out, later than their hands, but still before most people had poured their first cup of coffee. I sipped the stain from the bottom of my mug, left two quarters for a tip and was just straightening out my back when I heard the siren. Parsons and Fletcher looked up the street as one, and I hurried around the table to meet them. News.

"Fire?" I asked, peering up the highway. News was my job, but don't think I was happy about the prospects of a fire. A house or business fire was always a pity, and a forest fire… that would have been a catastrophe in those conditions.

"Guess so. The trucks pulled out and headed over the rise."

"Whose place is out that way?" Parsons asked, though he knew as well as anyone.

"Wheeler. Wheeler and Jake," Fletcher said. "You gonna go watch the fire, Bradford?"

But I was already fishing my keys out of my pocket. Once I was past the hill where the old church had stood, then around the bend and over the rise, I could see across the peaks of pines, maybe two miles out, a low streak like a swipe from a charcoal pencil drifting out along a ravine from behind a small mountain. The dust kicked up by the fire trucks still formed a haze which indicated the turn-off before I could see the road. With one hand I reached under the seat, trying to keep my eyes above the dash, and withdrew my camera. Cresting a small summit, I slowed to a roll, then came to a dead stop in order to get out and take a picture of the canyon below.

Not fire, but a swarm of mystical termites, locusts, beavers, glowing in frenzy, devoured the wild grass, the fallen trees, the juniper—not in one direction, but like a hole widening at the edges. No amount of training could have tipped the scales so much that the ten men breaking from the trucks would stand a chance.

It's that stinkin' Josh Jenkins. She didn't say so, but I know. She's been watchin' him at the baseball games all season. Can hardly peel her eyes off a him. I bet she told Rachel first, too. Tells her everything about us before she tells me. I'm like to read it in the newspaper 'fore I hear it from her. Fine! She wants him, she can have him. And he can have her, too, for all I care.

I hop down and duck in the passenger door to get that jacket I left in here. Ah, that's right! She took it after the last game. I sit out there on those butt-numbin' bleachers for hours watching her watch him play around in his tight white pants and then she goes off with my jacket when it wasn't even cool out. Yeah, he'll find that out, too, how she's always cold when it ain't cold and she don't bring back your jackets, neither.

Reminds me I gotta get my class ring back. Shoulda been the first thing she did, give my ring back. But she woulda had to face me to do that.

Gave her my ring. Hell, I only bought the damned thing so I could give it to her. What's a guy need a hunk a metal like that for 'cept to give it to a girl and let people know who gave it to her? And what all else? A necklace on Valentine's Day, but she can keep that. Throw it away for all I care. Fine by me. Stupid hearts. Chose it because a the gold hearts locked together like magician's rings. Guess she found a way to pull 'em apart, huh? Oh, they saw me comin'. Said, Here comes another high school boy thinks he found the girl he wants to marry, they said. Let's get out that stupid necklace with the stupid gold hearts, they said. Guess they got me.

Damn! What am I doin' shiverin' in July? Come on, Jack, get the furnace goin'! Ah! Like to knock you out, this stuff.

Know what? I got a better idea. Show her what she can do with her letter. I give her a necklace and my ring and she sticks a letter in my mailbox and doesn't even knock on the door to say it to my face? Show her what I think a that!

I rip up some a the brittle grass just off the dirt road, make a pile in one a the ruts. That's what this letter is good for: burnin'. Burn it up the way she done our love. Might as well grab a branch or two to throw on there since I'm gettin' it started, anyways. Warm up 'fore I head home. Don't wanna go back too soon and be home when she calls, though. Don't wanna talk to her. Guess there ain't no need for talk now that she told me what she thinks a me. Not worth the trouble—no, consideration—not worth the consideration to say it to my face, or just hand me the letter herself. That says a lot about a girl I gave a ring and necklace to—and I want that ring back. Even if I don't never find no one else to wear it, I want it back. Yeah, says a lot about a girl I thought I was gonna marry soon as I saved up some money from my first season on a Hot-Shot team.

Oh, come on now, Jack! Ah! That's the stuff.

Now where's them matches?

Aside from the monsters in the Sierra Nevadas, Sangre de Cristos, Bighorns, Laramies, and most all of Idaho, there were hundreds of brush fires sneaking around the country, engaging every smoke-jumper and air tanker we had hoped could come to our assistance. If we were going to stop the fire, we were going to have to do it ourselves.

If someone had just seen the flames earlier, it may not have been so bad. But whoever it was who was dumb enough to sneak into the forest and start a campfire was at least smart enough to hide behind a mountain. That alone might have lost us the fight. The flames were low, as was the smoke, slithering through the canyon until the wind finally brought it out where Jake Schepper saw its tail before he turned off toward his ranch. If he hadn't seen it then, who knows how much worse it might have been. Even so, it was already a mutant terror, creeping up the sides of opposing hills and trickling through two valleys, urged on by the fickle wind.

Someone from the valley, we figured. Those know-it-alls think we're just a bunch of hicks, and don't mind our speed limits, much less a chain across the forest road to let them know not to get in there.

A long folding table set unevenly on the ground, with a cooler of water placed near one end, and some papers, weighted down by a rock from the ground, their corners sporadically rattled by the furtive assaults of the wind, served as base camp on the level pasture just before the last rise above the valley where I first saw the fire. In town, businesses were locked up as citizens mobilized. A backhoe and two bulldozers were brought in from companies in town, and dozens of men fetched their chain saws when the fire chief told them they could clear the lower branches of the pines to prevent the fire from climbing the mature trees.

"Right now, the one bit of luck we've had is the fire is contained to the ground," Chief Turner told the men who stood before him with their chain saws hanging at their sides. "It's eating up fuel like grass and fallen branches, and moving slow enough we can catch it. But if it starts creeping up into the tall pines, and becomes a crown fire, that means it can hop and skip right over our heads all across the Mogollon Rim, and there's not much we can do about that without air support. So what you need to focus on is cutting away the lowest branches of the pines."

Raising the skirt, that's called. When I hear jargon, I have to get it explained so I can write it out for my readers. The men were assigned to groups of a half-dozen each, and given a leader with a radio. A few of the men had experience from being on smoke-chasing crews when they were younger, so these were mainly assigned as field officers, to coordinate the chain saw crews, fire break crews, and generally monitor the status of the fire.

You gotta believe me I didn't know I'd fall asleep. Just for a minute. I was just gonna get warm for a minute. I built the fire in one a the dirt ruts, deep as a pit, couple feet away from the grass, I swear. Oh, Jesus! When I woke and saw it sneakin' away into the forest, I tried to stop it, I swear! I didn't have no shovel so I just kicked dirt at it but there was more yellow grass than dirt and it was already seepin' out in every direction like a spilled drink. I had to give up and get outta there while I could, so I tore back over the hills into town. It was still dark, and I thought maybe I could just call the fire department and give them a tip, but I didn't want anyone to know it was me. Maybe they could trace the phone call, and even lift my fingerprints from the receiver, or match my voice, or who knows what. Oh, Lord, if they found out, how could I ever join the Hot-Shots?

I didn't sleep one minute last night, goin' back out to the front porch and lookin' to see if it had come over the ridge so I could see it. Even though there wasn't no glow and it was too dark to see smoke, I knew it was there and it was like the stars close to the horizon were a little dimmer, like the smoke was rising in front of 'em.

All morning I been waitin' for some news, for someone to come in with some news. I'm worried I'll say somethin' that I could only know if I was out there, and if they find out I was out there…

None a this woulda happened 'cept for that letter. I wouldn't a been out there, and I wouldn't a started no fire—Oh, Holy Jesus! Did the whole thing burn up? The letter! I don't know. I held it over the flames for a few seconds, but then it was too hot so I just dropped it in, but what if it didn't burn up? If there's just one corner a paper left, them fire investigation boys can piece it together, and they'll know I was out there. They'll find a fingerprint, or my tire tracks, or my name on a scrap a paper and they'll be puttin' my face on the front page as the kid who burnt down the whole country.

Oh, Lord, I gotta get back out there. Yeah! Yeah, that's it. If I get my truck out there today, they won't know last night's tracks from the new ones. And I'll work one a the crews makin' breaks so even if they do find out, I can say it was an accident and here at least I come down to take care of it.

"Mom!" I call from the patio, chain saw ready to go. She's just inside the kitchen 'cause I can hear the water running.

" What?" she says through the screens before opening the back door. When she sees me with the saw, I see her face twist like a scoldin's comin'.

"Mom, I'm gonna head on out there and help dad and the guys on the crews," I say.

"No, you are not going down there. One man from this family is enough. Now put that chain saw back in the shed."

But I say, "Mom, I gotta go help out."

"I don't want you getting hurt," she says.

"Mom, I'm gonna join the Hot-Shots next year, so this'll be good practice," I say, pleased with my lie.

"Over my dead body you're going to be a forest fire-fighter! Now do what I say. You can go out to base camp later with me and help serve up dinner, if you want to help."

I wonder if my mom would be so protective if she hadn't gone to nursing school. Anyways, she won't hear of it, so what can I do? Serve out dinner? No, that ain't gonna wipe the slate clean.

"We're keeping it out of the taller trees," Chief Turner told me. "But this wind is scattering the fire so much that it's more like three fires moving in different directions."

"Like fighting Cerberus," I said, imagining the typeset.

"What's that?"

"Title for the article I'm writing. One of them. I think I've got a whole edition of stories here."

"Just don't be getting in the way while you're writing your stories," Chief Turner said. His scorn was not even as substantial as the scent of the distant burn from atop that meadow. After sending the story out on the wire that night, I figured we'd have a whole litter of cub reporters from the big papers scurrying to get a piece of the action, and the media attention would bring the air support and man power we needed.

"Chief!" Someone too far off for me to recognize called through cupped hands, instead of using a radio, from the edge of the meadow which overlooked the fire. "Come look. I think we got trouble."

I accompanied Chief Turner as he jogged in his heavy boots over the deceptively bumpy ground. Though I'm not in great shape, I could have overtaken him, but I was careful to let him retain the lead. The lookout, Nelson Hunt, was using a pair of field glasses to track the progress of the flames. But the chief's fears were confirmed by a momentary survey with the naked eye.

"Damn wind's changed again," he said. "Who's down in that gully right now?"

"Uhm, Crew Three."

"All right. Radio them and tell them to get out."

But, as they would tell me in their exclusive interview, Crew Three did not get out so easily.

But she stands there in the doorway to watch me put the chain saw back. Why not just tell her? Ah, no. She'd tell someone. Dad for sure. This is too big for that. But I gotta get out there before they figure out who started that fire. And I need to take the chain saw with me, or else how am I gonna explain bein' out there? Think! Need to get Mom outta the house so I can get the saw and go without her stoppin' me.

I have a plan! I dial up my buddy Parker. "Parker, it's me. Hey, do me a favor, all right? Call me back in a second."

"Why? What's up?"

"Don't bother 'bout that. Just call me back."

When the phone rings, I call out, "I got it!" so my mom won't pick up the phone. After brushin' Parker off, I go into the kitchen to tell my mom, "That was Mrs. Ketchum from down the block. She wanted to know if you could go over to take a look at a mole she's got. Says she thinks it's skin cancer."

"Oh, that silly old woman. She's practically a hypochondriac. What am I? A doctor?"

"Well, anyways, I said sure, you'll be right over."

"Well, thank you very much, but don't speak for me in the future."

She washes her hands and I have a hard time waiting even that long until she finally leaves and I have to stand inside the front window to make sure she's past the neighbor's spruce and she can't see our yard anymore. Now I'd better hurry. She'll be there in a minute, and I do not want to get caught in a lie and a sneak. So I dash back to the shed, fumble that darned latch open, and snatch the saw, which I throw into the bed a my truck while the other hand is yankin' on the door handle. Don't even look down the street as I rip away 'cause if I see her comin' back toward me, wavin' her arm for me to stop and scowlin' at me and I have to ignore it, I'll be in even more trouble when this is all over.

Can't really see how much smoke there is until you come 'round the bend and over that rise and can see over the trees, down into the valleys. Just lying around like spilled ink. Up ahead I can see a state truck parked at the turnoff. Fella's got a radio in one hand, and waves me not to enter, but I pull in, anyways.

" Sorry, but you can't go in here. There's a fire down this road," he says. Figure he musta been called up from a Parks office somewhere, 'cause I never seen him before.

"I know. I'm bringin' this chain saw to my dad. One he took from home is the old one," I say, thumbin' to indicate the saw in the bed. "That old one has a bad motor. Like to seize up anytime."

My heart beats fifty times in the three seconds he takes to peer into the bed.

"All right. I'm gonna let you through, but stay on this road only, and stop when you get to the base camp up on the meadow. You can leave the saw with them, and they'll get it to your dad."

"Yessir," I say, trying not to dust him as I take off.

When Crew Three didn't emerge from the river of smoke after several minutes, Chief Turner had Nelson radio them again.

"We're on our way," the voice said, coughing before the speaker released the button.

But they still did not appear a few minutes later when a new voice came over the radio. "Bill's passed out. We're lost. We can't see two feet in front of us."

Even if we had had air support, no plane would have been able to locate them through that cloud as thick as oil. I could see Chief Turner trying to wring some solution out of the situation like water from a stone, but what could be done? "What's your position?" he said into the radio, perhaps not that he needed to know, but that he wanted the crew to know he was applying himself to the emergency.

"I told you, we can't see. Can't see up, can't see anything. It's dark as a cave in here. We been trying to follow the ravine out, but we shoulda been there by now."

"You boys keep down toward the ground. You'll be able to breathe better. Just keep moving," Turner said, then handed the radio back up to Nelson. "Keep talking to them. We gotta get them out of there before they all pass out from the smoke. Holy Jesus."

Turner was talking to the air by then, but his eyes were intent on something over my shoulder. Before I turned to look the Chief was by-stepping me, waving his arms over his head as he waltzed into the middle of the dirt road where a cloud like a snake was barreling toward us, a Chevy pick-up at its head. Turner put one hand out in front of him, signaling the truck to stop, and kept waving the other arm over his head. An avalanche of gravel accompanied the sudden stop as the tail of dust drifted forward past the truck before dissipating in the wind. Turner stepped around to the driver's window.

"What are you doing out here, son? You know you can't be around here now."

The boy inside seemed panicked. "I gotta get this saw to my dad," he said, as if it were an organ for a transplant.

"No, you can't be going any further. You just drop that saw off here, and I'll see he gets it."

"No, I gotta give it to him myself."

"Son, I am neck-deep in a crisis here, and I do not have time to argue with—"

But the boy had heard enough. He sprayed gravel so hard the chief had to turn his back and cover his face not to be bloodied.

"Dammit! Where the hell's he going?"

Unbelievable as it seemed, there was no other place to go but right into the smoke, into the fire. We watched helplessly as he careened down the slope, leveled out with no sign of letting up on the gas and plunged into the smoke, which swallowed him from our site. We could still hear the distant rev of the engine, though. He shifted, he fish-tailed, he skidded, then accelerated again. He bounded over rocks and logs as we peered toward the direction where the sounds buzzed out from the cloud like some insect we could not see. For several silent moments we waited to hear him crash headlong into a tree, and to this day I don't know how it is he avoided such a doom. There was a point when all fell quiet, but as we listened more carefully, we found that though the engine had lulled there was noise, indeed. Voices. Hollering and yelling, suddenly cut off as the engine once again revved, with a less reckless growl. We could clearly distinguish when it would emerge from the smoke, right back along the same trail it had followed in.

"We're out!" the radio in Nelson's hand blurted, but we could already see the men loaded in the back of the Chevy.

"Thank the Lord!" Turner said, suddenly sweating more than a moment before. "Looks like you got yourself a new headline."

I pulled the camera around on its strap and shot off half a roll as the truck climbed the slope, the men in the back whooping and swinging their hats over their heads, paramedics rushing up alongside, and through the ash on the windshield the beaming but stunned face of one teenage hero.

"I just knew I had to get down there and help," I say to that newspaper guy. Yeah, you take a good look at Josh Jenkins now, Sweetie. He ain't no hero gonna have his face sent "over the wire" to every newspaper in the country.

I knew the boy was hiding something, but what did it matter? He rushed in there yapping about taking a chain saw to his dad and ended up pulling out Crew Three, who were way off course and would have been dead, for sure. Which story did people want to read?

"Anyways, I just followed the road from memory. I know this forest like my own backyard. Fire didn't scare me. I'm gonna be a Hot-Shot next year, you know."

He could just as easily have run them down, with visibility as low as it was. Or crashed into a tree, giving his gas tank to the fire like a bon-bon. But that isn't what I wrote.

In the morning there'll be a new celebrity in America. In a few days the fire will be contained. The circumstances behind either won't much matter in the long run, as both will burn out and fade into memory.

Study in Darkness

Steady. All must be slow, careful, measured. A tiny flinch, an improper angle, a sudden jump could ruin it all. A steady grip, firm, yet not so tight that I might misdirect it by being too rigid. Slowly. I hold it level and calm. The trigger resists with even tension. In less than an instant, it will give way, letting the hammer fall. When it does…

My heart pauses in a weightless apex. A light tap at my temple.

That's three down, three to go.

I lay the pistol on the desk in front of me, side by side with my second weapon of choice. Vehemently powerful secrets dwell in both. In one, the secret revolves, its exact location maliciously surreptitious due to a sporting spin of the cylinder. In the other, the secret is said to be constant, though I dare anyone to say exactly where it lies. I will not rescind until I find one of these secrets. The only matter left to be decided is which one I will find first: which will save me from the other.

Just how does one come to the point of playing Russian roulette with deity? Was this match up in the making all my life? Or was it arranged in these last months, this very evening?

"I'm going for a walk," I said, not expecting a response. Her acerbic silence still injurious after thirty-two years. Still, it was less caustic than her words.

"'Live by the sword, die by the sword,' that's exactly what you said," she had accosted me.

"And that's what I meant. He knew what he was getting messed up in when he started his life of crime."

"Life of crime? He was sixteen, and had no prior arrests. Not everyone who walks into your courtroom is guilty."

"Yes! Yes, they are. They are all guilty. You just try and show me a guiltless man. Try!"

"Don't you know that the role of a judge is to apply his own reasoning and compassion to the circumstances? How can you do that when you are such a heartless monster?"

Far better to clutch my coat as I cast open the door, marching out briskly in no certain direction, than to be subject to the perusal of her eyes before which my every attempt to dissemble composure would have withered.

I turn on the desk lamp. We have no neighbors behind us, so I don't know why I bother switching it off every time I pick up the gun. No one's going to see me.

There's only a shot left in the first bottle, which I started into hours before I pulled out the weapons. One hand to pour the brandy, one to spread open the heavy leather cover of the book before me. I've read it all. Old and then New. Book by book. I've cross-referenced, analyzed, indexed, criticized, interpreted, and historicized. Exhaustively. I have done my homework. But I have never found the thing that transcends the words. This quality which millions of people across continents and through centuries have seized, I have never found. Tonight I will not embark on yet another research mission only to arrive at this impasse. Tonight the passages I peruse are random. Only luck will make the difference—or not. The book falls open, presenting First Corinthians, chapter two, calmly and deliberately, just like with the revolver. Rules of the game. Level playing field, as it were. One page of scripture for each bullet. The brandy is just a mediator. A shot of courage, you might say. Compared to resolve, courage is only temporary blindness. I open the book and read the page. If it is embodied with some spiritual essence beyond the words, you win. If not, I take a turn with the gun.

Oh, these epistles from Paul are exemplary of ancient rhetoric. Worthy of careful study, to be certain. But how contrived could your rebuttal be? Oh, there it lurks, at the end, as if to snare me. Shall I quote it back to you? "The spiritual man makes judgments about all things, but he himself is not subject to any man's judgment."

Oh, please. You have so much at your disposal, and this is how you plan to convert me? You may want to consider a less direct approach. We both know that I am no spiritual man. If I were, this little challenge wouldn't be necessary. But let me tell you this, as well, I am above other men's judgment. Oh, I have sinned. I can count them out for you. But I have paid for everything I have ever done. Though my wife protests, that is exactly what makes me fit to judge: I am guiltless. And perhaps that's why I can't find you. Because I don't need you. All these sheep, they only come crying to you when they have risked their seat in your eternal cathedral. Well, I don't have that weakness, so how can you entice me?

These words hold no epiphany: no affirmation for my soul.

The brandy burns comfortably along the back of my throat. Again the exchange of weapons. Again the coolness, the heft, the control. Colt Single Action Army, Ainsworth Cavalry Model. Collectors would shriek to find I've loaded it, am dry-firing it. But if anyone ever finds out, I won't be around to suffer their outrage. The barrel has been cut to only five inches, probably after it was salvaged from some battle, allowing a level aim without contorting my wrist. My great-great-grandfather with the 5th Cavalry hunted Geronimo in the southern Arizona Territory with a gun like this. This one was bought at auction, as was the Bible. No family frontier Bible found its way through the generations to me. If there ever were such a thing, it must have gone to one of the aunts long ago. Maybe it has been sold in auction to some collector back east. Maybe it was the only one imbued with the essence I'm looking for.

I switch off the light, release the glass on the desk, reach for the gun, cognizant of its location though I can not see. The odds are increasing now, aren't they? You don't have much time left to open my eyes to your little secret, do you?

Steady. Steady. I breathe out, pause, pull the trigger.

Oh! So you want to go another round?

As I turn the lamp back on, I consider spreading my cleaning kit across the desk to offer the police and reporters a polite obituary: "Accidental death while cleaning firearm." The last thing I would want to do is make a stain on the front page and embarrass our governor. The same governor who will not be re-appointing me now that this has all come to light.

" Look, your term is almost up, and public opinion has changed since you originally took the bench. No matter how much the governor supports you, she needs to appoint judges who reflect her commitment to her constituency. There's a good chance this upstart Chavez might give you a run for your money."

That's what the "political consultant" came up from the valley to tell me in person, on behalf of the governor. That was the root of this evil.

"It's not about image: it's about looking into those thieving hearts and knowing when someone is lying to you," I told him. "My great grandfather and his brother both wore the robe, and then my grandfather, my father, and now me. It's in our blood."

"I'm not saying you have to change your politics. But it wouldn't hurt if you were to throw the public a bone. Show them your compassionate side. Look, you've always been tough on juvenile offenders. That's just common knowledge around here. Now, you've got two cases in particular on your docket this week and I think it would do a lot for your image if you were to be lenient."

"Be lenient? Go soft, you mean. You want me to set these punks free because the people are soft-headed? Don't you think voters can smell when a politician changes his stripes. If I start setting hooligans free now, it's going to do more harm than good."

"All right," he said. He scratched his chin as if to ponder a question, but I could see the gesture was rehearsed, the decision previously made. "You're right. So let's not set them both free. Just one. Take it easy on one, and play your usual hardball with the other. That's exactly what we need. It'll let your supporters know you're still sticking by your guns, but it'll also suggest that you aren't just blindly putting these kids away."

"Just agree to let one of them go? To satisfy the bleeding hearts?"

"Bleeding hearts who vote."

The only question left was which one should it be? Toby Martin was a local kid whose file I had read before. Consistent foolishness. Shoplifting, joyriding. But he was popular in the community. Did I ever expect him to straighten up? No. But neither did I expect him to ever harm anyone. He was just a good kid from a good family who did stupid things and tended to get caught.

Now this other kid, he was from down in Tempe, up here with some buddies over the weekend. I could see it in his face when he appeared before me, no matter what his file said. "No prior arrests" does not mean he had never broken the law. Oh, those punks can fool those ignorant cops in the city, most of whom are breaking more laws than they're enforcing, anyway. But when he appeared before me, I could look right down past those innocent pupils into the sinful core of that boy.

Was there any choice? I let the Martin boy go and delivered overdue justice to that spoiled valley snot.

The Gospel of John, chapter nine. Oh, come on. Are you using a stacked deck? "For judgment?" Oh, was that why you were here? Me, too! Me, too. Ha! The blind will see, and those who see will become blind. Yes, I know. And the last shall be called first, and beggars will become kings. Of course, of course.

What do you want from me? To give you my money? The house and cars and country club membership? Could it be so easy? I hardly think so. If I thought for a moment it would do the trick, I would cash it all in and put it in the collection plate. But don't try to tell me that every rich person is rotten and every poor person pure. Such simplicity! Can I be baptized and let the water work the change? If I go to church every Sunday, twice on Easter, will I inhale it from the incense fumes and votive candles? Don't you see that these parlor tricks are transparent to me?

I close the book with one hand, then open the second bottle of brandy. I pour a finger, then turn off the lamp before I tilt my head back to drink. Setting down the glass, my hand hovers over the dark desk to rest on the gun momentarily before slipping into its contour and raising it up. It won't be long now.

I hold it steadily, evenly against my head. The trigger, the swan dive of my heart in the moment the limit of tension is surpassed and the hammer is launched. Only to strike harmlessly above the empty chamber.

He died. I wouldn't have remembered his name, except for the persistent headlines and calls from reporters. He got caught up in the middle of an ongoing feud between long-term detainees and was killed in the county jail, killing my career. Oh, no one cared about me in the least, except that I was a way to target the governor. Never mind the ruin that would be strewn about me. Never mind that she would see those articles.

"I just don't understand why you let him be tried as an adult," she said.

"It was a judicial decision," I told her.

"But he was seventeen."

"That's right. Seventeen and seven months old. That's old enough to know what he was doing."

She read those articles each morning, right in front of me at the table.

"It says that he didn't even have a criminal record. That was his first offense."

"Yes, I know. Don't you think I know? I heard the case, as I recall." Who was she to challenge my judgment? Was it given to her lineage to see into the hearts of men?

But she would persist until the point that I would take a driven walk through the crisp evening, not returning until she was asleep. Was she accusing me? A "heartless monster" she called me. What does she know? Does she know that I sent the Martin boy home to his parents? There is my compassion! Generosity, leniency, grace! And they dare to blame me for that Tempe boy's death?

Your final breath. Famous last words?

The spine divides, presenting the Gospel of Mark, chapter eight. Oh, and I see you intend to give me a fight at the end. Am I the Pharisee asking for a sign? Is this the wicked and adulterous generation to whom no sign shall be given? Yes, I know this trap you have laid, but I can do you one better. Give me a moment… I can find it… Yes! Isaiah 7:11. "Ask the Lord your God for a sign, whether in the deepest depths or in the highest heights."

So why not me? Is it only your chosen ones who are good enough for reassurance? Why do they all have it? The understanding? Why not me? My wife… was just "hit" by it, she said. From out of nowhere it just soared down and "hit" her, like pigeon droppings! Is it genetic? If so, is it the Believer or the Heretic who needs therapy? Hereditary? But my forefathers were as steadfast as hers. No. This condition started—or ended—with me.

Where is my soul?

Thoughts liquefy, then ignite in indignation, and I can not remain still. The fairness! Where is the fairness? Where is the law, so carefully prescribed to, either natural or spiritual law, that determines who gets it? I have judged in fairness! I have judged men in fairness behind the bench for all these years, and I deserve my share in return, you so-called God of righteousness.

Rising, I leave the weapons, the issue, behind. Out to the glass wall of the Arizona room, where the moonless night is a ceiling and wall of a billion gallons of crude, crude oil pressing down. Moonless, starless, Godless night. The brightness of the single desk lamp against the inside of the window obscures the depths of the entire universe from my eyes. I wipe my hand across the suspended condensation. One quarter of an inch from my fingertips is the patio I can't see, which I only suppose exists as it should because it has remained the same way for years, bordered by shrubs and a modest lawn, then the sudden wilderness. But in the quarter inch, an impenetrable barrier. If I cupped my hands around my eyes and pressed my face to the glass, details might solidify, but I can't reach out and know for certain. Then again, what could be there? Couldn't it truly be the fathoms of liquid darkness? Couldn't it be a mountain lion, or pack of wolves? Couldn't it be some insanely calculating, finally desperate madman straining to see me, his target, just as I strain to see him? My finger skates along the slippery face in ornate cursive loops. "God," it traces.

Knowing without seeing, I enter the bedroom. I know her face is soft, relaxed. Her breath comes easily. How can she be so serene when she doesn't know any more than I do what's out there right now? On her face is the satisfaction of a secret anyone would love to know. Is that smugness? No. I would be one to gloat about it: not her. She would tell me if she only could.

But I know that she can't explain this thing. Still, her heart is one that would give up anything asked of it. If only I could ask. Pride. Pride, pride, pride, pride, pride. I am a proud man: she knew that long before we even spoke of marriage. But maybe she expected to rid me of that. Well, why should I let her? When it's all said and done, pride's all a man has in this world.

Passing back through the Arizona room I wipe my hand along the moist glass, erasing all signs of deity.

Well, it was a good game, wasn't it? But in the end, you lost. You proved nothing to me. You didn't prove what can't be proven because it—you—doesn't exist. But I saved a little surprise for you. That's right. See, I didn't think you were going to just descend in a pillar of light. Not for me. You wouldn't even send an angel for me, would you? So this is what it comes to. I have to come up there myself.

You think I won't do it? Well I'm going to prove you wrong right here, tonight, Mister. This is number six, and we both know what that means: This is the one. Oh, you saved it for the end, trying to draw out the drama maybe or trying to make me lose my nerve, but here I am, and I am resolved to this.

I suppose I have time for one more drink, though. A toast to the winner. Hell, why am I even talking to you? You've just proven you aren't there. Hey, don't get upset about it, I played by the rules, and I won fair and square. To be honest, I expected more out of you.

Wait. Wait, wait, wait. I have to think. Maybe I shouldn't do this here. I don't want her to come out and find my blood all over the room. I could just drive up the mountain a ways, and do it where no one would have to clean up the mess. No. No, if

I get in the car who knows what might happen. What if I am pulled over, or have an accident? This has to be settled here and now. Right. All right, but outside. So I turn off the lamp and feel my way along the wall to the sliding door of the Arizona room. Outside, the darkness assumes its depth, retreats into murky ranks of patio furniture, shrubs, trees. At the edge of the forest I stop. Here. This is far enough. No, I'm not shaking from nerves. You'd like to think so. It just gets chilly at this elevation at night. No, I'm steady as a rock. It's you who should be shaking, because I am about to march out of this human shell and expose you once and for all. Exhale. Steady. I close my eyes, raise the gun. Where is it? I feel it now. I feel it. Against my temple. Steady… breathe steady. I pull the trigger.

The tap at my temple is not what I expect. How can this be? I know I counted six. This is the sixth chamber of a six-shooter. No! No, you aren't going to cheat. I won. You do not exist. I won. This is a mechanical failure. I should have used a newer gun.

I put the barrel back to my head, pull the trigger again, but again there is only the clacking sound of the hammer. Without moving, I draw in breath, steel my frame. Again! Again! A full six times without interruption. Still the bullet eludes me. Six more times, and nothing. You're cheating! I loaded this gun myself!

I lower the gun right in front of my face, squint in the absence of light, but can see nothing, so I return to the study, stumbling across the level patio. Under the lamp light, I find the single bullet just where it should be. I extract it, examine it to be sure it is in good shape. What is wrong with this piece of junk? I insert the bullet into a new chamber, line it up so it will be the first to fire, and turn off the lamp and close the door behind me as I return to the edge of the forest.

What kind of a god goes around breaking the rules?

Again the steady pose, the trigger. And again no thunder. I pull the trigger five times, place the gun back to my temple and pull it the sixth, but nothing.

You're cheating! I'll get another gun! I'll find another way!

I lower the barrel toward the ground and harass the trigger like flicking a lighter that won't light. Damn it, damn it, damn it, damn it, damn it, damn it! But on the sixth try the bullet fires, making the empty void cringe against the advance of sound.

Her shriek pierces the window. The gun makes no sound as it falls from my grasp. Nearly crashing through the sliding door, I tunnel through the Arizona room, enter the bedroom to find her clutching the covers to her heart.

"Oh, Lord! What was that?" she says, weeping a blend of fear and relief.

"A thief," I say. I cradle her in my arms and rock back and forth with her, brushing her hair from her ear. "He was trying to get in through the patio door."

"Did you shoot him?" she asks, then trembles and reiterates. "Did you kill him?"

"No," I say, "I just scared him off."

His Two Hearts

The distance is among them.

Sitting in the car, traversing darkness wider than Wyoming skies, he has long since been aware that distance is a state of mind. He would rather be driving. He would rather be alone. Isolation not an option, he feigns exhaustion, which at least garners him the silence in which to wonder what she would be doing at that moment.

Remoteness is not isolation. Remoteness is seeing the lights of homes at the foot of mountains so dark that no perception of depth is allowed: the only way to know of the behemoth's presence the silhouette it carves in the otherwise starry sky. Remoteness is driving across the vast Arizona high desert and seeing only the lights from a town under this mountain range too dark to name, and knowing you won't be going even there. Knowing that your own porch light hides along a lane in a valley through a tunnel beyond a range beyond the plains which await over the ridge before you. This is the mournful tranquility he longs for. When he has the chance to drive alone, he will take advantage of the jet lag and return to a rise such as this, pull onto the shoulder, walk away from the cooling engine, let his eyes adjust to the blue and silver hues under the waning moon's glow, and enjoy the minor stirrings of the suspended coolness.

From the crest of any hill there is a light or a swarm of lights which may as well be stars, so far away they are reduced to a twinkling singularity; and you can not be sure whether that light has only traversed the depth of land or if it speaks from an entirely separate moment, a predecessor of the one in which you ponder whether you could ever reach those lights before dawn dissipated them like phantoms.

The steering wheel vibrates so subtly that his mother's hands don't shake, but only the inside of her grip grows weary against the lullaby hum.

"You want me to drive?" he asks.

"No. You should get some rest, kiddo," she says, content in being his mother again.

Ahead of them a crumb trail of street lights leads to store lights, and the radiant open air luminescence of a four island, twenty-four pump Shell station. Yellow makes it all the brighter. The moths can be heard against the plastic diffusers overhead. Before the scent of gasoline falls behind them, he is asleep.

How he got to be here is no more the story of a taxi, airplane, and going through customs than love is the tale of a dozen roses presented at the door on a first date.

Liftoff. An ocean, one bag of honey-roasted peanuts, two orange juices, two in-flight movies, four plastic cups of water, eight time zones, forty-seven pages of a novel with sparse dialog, six thousand miles. Another runway. Then a couple of hours in the LAX terminal, home to overpriced delis and news stands. The second flight, like a school bus ride in comparison.

If a forest is six thousand miles wide, and you walk through it at the speed of sound for 10 hours, how far into the forest did you go? It's a trick question: you can only go three thousand miles in, and then you're going out again.

" Sleep well?" his step-father asks as he emerges from the bedroom, bypasses the bathroom and heads through the living room on his way to the kitchen. His own father is dead, buried fourteen hundred miles and six feet away, not lamented for. So why still define this one, the one who took him in without ever meeting him, as a "step?" Something young and no longer malleable demands classification.

"I feel like my head's stuck in tar. I've been rolling in and out of sleep for hours," he says, continuing into the kitchen, talking over the refrigerator door as he scans the contents. He doesn't want more orange juice, having lost his immediate taste for it on the plane and in LAX. But water is too bland to combat the film in his mouth. An international film. So he bends down for the milk.

His dad—but there is a pang to attach the classifying tag—listens to the Weather Channel while re-reading an Asimov novel. "There's some leftovers in there, I think. Maybe some tacos, or chicken?"

He looks at the clock over the door to find it is early afternoon, then automatically calculates the time in Seoul. Early morning of the next day. Still, his stomach declares it is morning, and insists on appropriate food. So he pours a bowl of Raisin Bran, which has probably been here since his last trip home. Only his (half-)brother eats cereal around here, and only cereal meant for elementary school kids, though he is in high school.

"So, how are things going over there?" his dad asks as he sits down with his dry cereal on the couch. "Jinny all right?"

"She's fine. We're doing fine," he says. He knows that the question is genuine, and that his dad finds it hard to say genuine things, unless they express anger. Even then, you only get the eruption, and have to divine the source for yourself. Fathers are like that.

Jinny is a pretty fair representation of her name in English, and he never bothers to make an effort to say it more authentically to her, though he wonders now if saying it so would sound more like "I love you" than "I love you" does in translation.

"Yeah, we're fine. Wish I could see more of her, but her job keeps her pretty occupied. I swear, the working conditions there are criminal. They use their workers like property."

"When's she gonna come over so you can introduce us?"

"Good question. It's not easy for her to get time off, and the trip takes so long. But maybe next summer, I hope." He had hoped that last summer and in the winter, too. He canceled his trip last year once it was certain Jinny could not accompany him, but he couldn't cancel again. After all, they aren't even married yet, and here he has a family waiting to see him whenever he can make the flight over. He has to leave her from time to time, in order to be here.

He does not miss Seoul. Especially in the summer. The air there is a shirtless, hirsute man moist with watermelon juice sticky sweat who hugs you and licks you and as soon as you shower he is at it again. But here, in the middle of the day, shooting at cans and an old cast iron bathtub someone had rolled out of the bed of a truck and into the sand, the heat leaves no mark, except thirst.

His brother wields the larger gun, shoots more rounds, aims with less precision. It is their relationship, not their bloodline, which merits the classifying "half-." But it is only a visit, so they put aside differences. Maybe they've even grown past whatever grew between them, but neither is eager to scrutinize the situation.

"Hey!" he calls between shots. When his brother lowers the rifle and turns his head, he continues, "I'm going to climb up that slope and get some pictures! Don't shoot me!"

"All right!" his brother calls back. Still, he worries faintly.

Wherever he goes, this is what he does: takes pictures to take back, not for his own pleasure but to show her what she couldn't go see for herself. So he climbs the crumbling-beneath-his-steps slope, skids once, not falling down, resumes course for a patch of cacti in bloom. And the horizon. No buildings as far as the lens can see. No, he does not miss Seoul.

He misses her passively, knowing there's nothing he can do about it, knowing she'll be there when he returns. His biggest fear is not dying in a plane crash: it is that he would die in a plane crash and she would not know that he was on his way back to see her—that she would think he abandoned her.

"But what would you do if you met a really pretty American woman?" she pressed.

"I'd look at her," he teased. She is beautiful. Her beauty warms his blood, elicits sighs, literally makes his heart leap when he thanks God for her in his prayers at night.

"Would you think about leaving me?"

"You think some woman, just because she's American, could make me think that? Honey, I could quit my job any time I want and get on a plane and leave Korea. But I'm still here, aren't I? So that must not be what I want."

She knows he hates his job.

His mother and he steal the car and make a break for Chiricahua, which he knows how to pronounce, and still mispronounces nearly every time he says it, until he finally decides not to try to get it right. He has her stop so he can take a picture of a pair of buzzards on log fence posts, but one flies away before he has the camera ready.

They drive the car through the park, stop at the interesting points, see some birds, feel the heat. She talks about "Someday I'd like to take a whole weekend and just drive that road back there and see where I end up. Explore."

He knows she's serious, and would offer to pay for the gas, but knows she has to work the next day.

"Look at this lizard," he says, up the trail. They don't hike far. She's not in shape for it. "I've never seen one like this. It's sort of copper colored."

"Let's stop at the gift shop on the way out and see if they have a book," she suggests.

When he asks her to take his picture, she doesn't expect that he'd make such an event out of it. Yes, she did know. As he cuts back and forth across the snaggly growth and rocks, she fiddles with the camera, zooms in and out on a few targets. "You think you can get me in the frame and those formations over there, too?" he calls back.

“What? I can’t hear you.” He is on top of a massive rock with nothing behind him except the valley and the opposite mountain.

They picnic near a stream bed with little water in it before they leave the park, having flipped through several books but buying none. No other cars in the pull-off parking lot, they relax at a picnic table in the shade, listen to the unidentifiable bird chirps. “Maybe we should have bought one of those books, after all,” she says.

“Why? They don’t have audio.”

“Noooo… but we could try to see what birds are making those sounds, and then match them with a picture.” She doesn’t mind his smart-ass remarks, knowing they are never intended harmfully, and overlooking the less humorous ones.

They pack the cooler back into the car, grab the camera, and walk along the path beside the creek bed, but can see no birds for all the brush.

Despite the perfectly blue sky, they meet a downpour on the way home, then emerge from it with forty-five minutes left to drive. That stretch is the same as the other night, coming down from Tucson. This time it is less like going home and more like cutting a trip short.

He drives. Arizona floats by like islands. Picacho Peak. His favorite landmark. He takes pictures. Stops to see folks in Tucson, then continues through Tempe, where another aunt lives, and onto Flagstaff, to meet friends and head to Lake Powell, where he is stunned anew by the marvelous grandeur of this place. After nearly two weeks on the road, he returns home, having made the rounds, seen the sights, taken just shy of a hundred pictures.

A single archetypal exchange epitomizes visits with aunts, grandma, and friends:

"So, when are you going to get a job back here so we can see more of you?" Never mind that some of them actually see him more often now, once a year, than they did before he left the country.

"Well, if things go right, we'll see about getting married in another year, I think. Then I guess we'll spend a few more years there before having children. I want them to go to school here, though. So we'll move back here before then."

"So… not too soon, huh?"

To his friends, but not family, he explains, "I'd just marry her and come back and buy a house, if it were that simple. But we have to be completely sure about everything, because there's a lot of complications. Countries, cultures, families, futures."

To his closest friends only, he confides, "I don't want her to come over here and decide she can't take it and leave me."

When he is awake at three in the morning, sitting on the porch swing out back, hoping the creaking it makes is not loud enough to wake anyone, he looks up at that stars he misses so much in Seoul, where there is too much light, too much dirt in the air to see much more than the moon. Astronomy was almost his minor, was his hobby, and is one of his loves. He loves nothing about astro-physics: everything about constellations and expeditions to the moon and Mars as imagined by authors like Ray Bradbury. They have lain on their backs on a blanket on the front lawn, sprawled in sundry orientations, his mother and (half-)brothers and sister and he, and counted shooting stars during the Perseid shower. This he cannot do in Seoul.

He tells her stories about the red rocks in Sedona, the aspens north of Flagstaff, the antelope, elk, and deer, the air and space and wondrous expanses. Trying to sell her on it? No, she wants to come. They want to come. When they can.

Thoughts of her more numerous than the stars. Worries, hopes, memories, desire, longing. Six thousand miles and change, but he feels less removed from her than from the family whose house he sleeps in. Home is where the heart is? You can't go home again? There's no place like home, home on the range.

Another plane will inhale him through that straw to the terminal, let him settle in its belly. Knowing he can't see anyone in the terminal through his window, he will stop trying after a moment, pull a book from his bag for this first, short flight. In the bottom of his lungs, hidden from the x-ray machine, so far down he can't feel it, but knows it is there, lies a terrificly condensed swallow of air from home. Maybe he will release when they kiss upon seeing each other for the first time in four weeks, and let her know that all his stories, all the times he says things are different there, are true. Or maybe he will treasure it longer. Someday, when the smog mobilizes and assaults him en force, he can release that gasp, and it will either save him or make his last breath a breath from home.

He grins at his own melodrama.

The plane thrusts forward, upward. Gravity hollers for him from below. He feels the tension of one rubber band around him as it is pulled tight and stretches, and the relaxing of another as it is slackened reciprocally.

Nothing But Infinity

When you stand out here on a moonless night, there's not much you can't see. The truck stop sign flashing the time and temperature between specials and cigarette prices. The spire of the Main Street Chapel illuminated from below by amber lights. Glowing eyes of the cars, humming on the interstate. And more. The sky. Stars forever and as far as we can see. Even with telescopes. Nothing but infinity. And time. They say that by the time light from some of the most distant stars reaches Earth that it's millions of years old. Billions of years, even. Like looking back in time.

I just got home from the movie. I go three times a week, sometimes more, alone. Twenty-five years ago, when the theater was new, I went about once every two weeks, hardly ever without a date. Things change.

I was born here. Not too long ago, I decided that I would die here. Most of my friends have moved away. But their families are still here, and someday they, too, will return. Like a black hole way out there in space, it pulls you back, this town. When I got out, I thought it was for good… and for my good, too. Went to school, piddled around, got married, went back to school. I was a pharmacist in a franchise drug store for ten years before I was able to buy my own branch store. My wife and I moved to Phoenix, where my store was.

Debra couldn't have kids. She had two miscarriages before we knew. The first time, she cried all night after it aborted. Calming her was impossible, but I stayed up and talked to her. It wasn't helping any, but that's the way life goes: Sometimes you just need to keep trying, keep hoping, even when the futility of the effort is imminent.

Our house was behind the store, facing the street on the opposite side of the block. The building had housed an automobile parts store. The discount place down the street put it out of business, they say. Big as a parking lot and empty as the future. We moved toiletries, electronics, magazines, diapers, office supplies, candy, and other money makers into the store and onto our new shelves and racks. My pharmacy sat on a platform raised two feet and I could see over all the aisles. It was mine, I had made it, and it was good.

Grand opening wasn't much of a success. What was there to be excited about? Must've been a hundred drug stores in town already, having sales every week. But business picked up and stayed steady.

A couple of years later, the gangs became a problem. They hadn't invaded our neighborhood, yet, but they were close. Four blocks down there'd been a stabbing. Two blocks over, a shooting. It was good when we moved there, but the territories were always expanding. Things change.

I worked ten hour days. From ten until eight, and took the paperwork home, sometimes. One night, quarter before closing, this boy walks into my store. There's no one else around...no customers, and Jonie, my clerk, she's stocking cosmetics. I stand at my counter and pretend to read a magazine which I pulled from the rack. It's a month old, and I'm not interested in it. I'm interested in this kid. He's got on a bulky jacket, army green, and ripped-up jeans. He's holding one arm across his stomach, the hand enveloped by the green jacket on the other side. Could have a gun. Walking funny, too, like maybe he's drunk or on something. Probably here to stick me up, make off with some pain killers. I knew it would happen sooner or later. I stay calm, looking at the magazine, but watching the kid. He comes to the aisle right in front of my counter. Passes me. Passes the condoms, passes the vitamins, the brand name medicine. But stops at the first aid supplies.

He knows I'm right behind him. Knows I can see the gauze, the antiseptic he's piling into his coat and the arm across his stomach. I put the magazine on the counter and go around to the swinging door, step down, and wait for him at the mouth of the aisle. He doesn't need to look, he knows where I am. He walks to the end of the shelving unit, halfway down the length of my store, turns and moves toward the side where Jonie is shelving facial cream. I walk along the top of the aisle with him, eyes locked on him. I won't tolerate stealing from my store. He reaches the last aisle, where Jonie is. She sees him, smiles. She doesn't know what's going on. He looks at me, not as a challenge, not as a threat. He is announcing his departure. That is all.

Our eyes are locked as he walks up the aisle, cautiously, but firmly, even though his gait wavers some. My hands slip from my hips and I suppose my stance looks like a gunfighter waiting to draw. Just comes up the aisle like he were receiving communion. Then, not in a frantic rush, not as a sudden bolting action, but simply like stepping around someone on the sidewalk, he tries to walk past me.

"Not so fast, you thief," I say. "All right, empty your pockets."

He just stares at me. Doesn't say anything. Then he tries to get past: not violently, but resolutely. I grab his arm by the shoulder, the arm that is holding his stomach. This pulls the arm away. I see it. Blood, matted and drying there from the wound in his torso. He is standing at his own arm's length from me, still staring at my eyes, past my eyes, at me. At what I am. Asking me questions both philosophical and moral and ethical.

Just stares at me with eyes that are neither sad nor angry, not cold, not insane. Eyes that say I am ready for anything, and I will handle it. They say I need to go. But not "please." They do not need to beg of anyone...they will not beg. These eyes that are talking to me of so many things that I can never understand because I have been lucky enough to never have to face those tests. Eyes to which I can not respond.

I let him go and watch him leave the store as nonchalantly as any paying customer.

When I was young, living out here. I'd wish on the stars. Thousands of wishes. Thousands. They never came true. Maybe it was how I did it, maybe I got a few of the words mixed up, so it nullified the wish. Maybe, somehow, I knew that they wouldn't come true anyway. Somehow I knew, and if I knew that, they never could. Just stars. Just me. Just foolish wishes wasted.

Time to go in. I'll sit up for a while longer. Turn on the television, but not watch it. Glance at the paper, brush my teeth. Fall asleep listening to the radio station that plays music from my era. Songs that whisper and croon about dreams and loves and times I never had. Songs that lull me to sleep with anything but the truth.

How do I spend my days? I wish I knew. I rise early, often take a walk, go back to bed until the sun has begun warming the land. Turn on the television in the morning, but don't watch it. Shower. Fill the bird feeder, pull a few weeds from the flower beds which have no flowers. Write a letter which is long overdue even though I have no excuse to not write. Tinker with something around the house. But mostly I go into town. I sit at the counter in the café when I can't find a booth. Read magazines. Fiction. Not the news. Go to the library, look at books. That's where I read about the stars. About time, and how it's still there for us to look at even billions of years after it is nothing. Like a sorcerer searching for a lost spell, I pore over volumes as if they could restore the essence I let vanish by not believing in one Book when I had the chance.

I sold the store. I'm retired. Too early, some tell me. Too early, I think, but far too late, I know. I have rentals in the valley that let me live comfortably. But there is nothing in which I want to indulge. All is vanity. And yet my days here are not over.

That boy came in often. The same thing each time, only I never again tried to stop him. No hesitation, right to the first aid supplies. No words spoken, but always eye contact. Always those same eyes. What if it had been someone else with the boy —someone who didn't see what was there, who tried to stop him? I don't know if he would have fought for freedom, or accepted apprehension. When I really think about it, I see him walking on, like a force of nature (No, more powerful than that. Like knowledge. Pure, irrefutable, unstoppable, irrevocable knowledge!), not evading capture, but overcoming it. And not overcoming it by physical or violent force, but by a strength that can only be called righteousness. A power to render mountains asunder. How was he born with something I've searched so long to acquire?

I told my wife about the first time. She was scared for me and wanted to move, I think. It really shook her up. I knew what had happened. Or at least I thought I knew. Probably a fight, or an initiation. Anyhow, he needed those things, and I had no right to deny him. When had I ever been turned down in my life? When had my survival ever hung in the balance of anything? When had Death done more than tease me by taking someone I knew?

Debra was diagnosed with cancer five years ago. She hadn't been examined as regularly as she should have been, and it might be too late, the doctor said. It was. They operated and did what they could, but it wasn't enough. Debra died just over a year ago.

After the library, I come home to eat, or stay in town and walk around. A few times, I've visited families I knew before I left.

Whatever I feel like. It's a ten minute drive from my house to the theater, and most everything else in town for that matter, since downtown is a nucleus in size, compared to the dispersed residences. My house is in a small area of development west of town. Across the highway is a wheat field. Down the road a bit is a cattle ranch. And nothing else until the interstate.

The movie tonight was sad. It was about these lovers who parted because of a misunderstanding. They had the real thing. Love. That's the one consolation I have in Debra's death: We stayed together until the end. I've known people who divorced. It isn't easy for them. Two years, ten years, twenty years later, I can still see the pain. They say that their lives are going fine now. Must have been a mistake in the first place. No harm done. You forget about it after awhile.

Lies. I can see into them like that boy saw into me. I can see the hurting that will never stop, so they have to stop thinking about it instead. Like that boy.

He came in for months. Almost two years, actually. Always the same. Then, one time, it was someone else. A different body walked in. A little shorter, longer hair, and lighter skin. Another boy doing the same thing and getting the same treatment from me. Because it was him. Different body. Same soul. This soul belonged to this new body as much as it had to the other. It lent itself to thousands. They needed it to stay alive and stay sane.

This new boy with the timeless soul looked into my eyes. No apprehension. No fear. All understanding.

After the movie, I drove on the interstate for awhile, then on a deserted back road. By the time I pulled in at home, it was nearly two. And there was a tremendous, white cow in my front yard. I didn't know how it got there, but I knew where it came from: the ranch up the road. When the engine stopped, the cow took off at a quick pace. Not knowing the name of the rancher, I called the Humane Society. They said they'd be out to retrieve the cow. I wasn't sleepy—I'm never sleepy anymore, just tired —so I left the porch light on and opened the curtains, and waited for them to arrive. It took awhile, and I ceased to anticipate their appearance, so I proceeded to change into my nightclothes. I saw two trucks pull onto my street and I went outside. I could hear them talking, determining which way the cow went, and how to deal with it. I wanted to help, so I started walking toward the trucks. Before I was out of my driveway, the trucks pulled back onto my street and headed toward the cul de sac. I stopped and sat on the brick column at the mouth of my driveway.

How ridiculous I looked, if anyone saw, sitting there, waving my arms now and then, giving directions to the officers who were as unaware of my presence as I had been of sorrow. An aging man in his robe, his bare feet brushing the grass, eyes intent upon two trucks at the end of the road. Futile. How ridiculous we must look, screaming and crying, hoping and praying, always when it's too late. Futile.

I went inside, but left the porch light on in case they needed to speak to someone.

Debra died painlessly, they say. I know better. There is no way in hell that you can spend four years waiting for death, looking back on your life, wishing you had been able to raise a family, and die painlessly. She cried often. I never cried where she could see me. She had to believe that I was strong—as if that would solve the problem, cure her cancer. But, when alone, before coming home from the store at night, I'd sit in my office and cry. Just cry until it couldn't come out anymore. I'd ask God questions I knew he wasn't going to answer. And cry.

That boy, the one who started it all, was dead, of course. At this am not merely guessing. I saw his body. It was on the news one night...the first night the new boy came into the store. Someone had a video recorder handy and recorded it. A fight, some fists and knives, but mostly guns. The tape was dark. Now and then a flash from a pistol would show up, the sound came just after. The camera operator zoomed in and out of the action with the twist of a knob. Once, the camera rushed to meet the face of a young man who was standing under a streetlight, who was about to be shot in the chest by a pump action shotgun. It was him. No fear, no pain. Consummate awareness and understanding.

That boy had no more answers to life's questions than any of us, but he knew enough to quit asking them.

Now and then I think foolishly. We all do. No matter how many trials I face, I always think that it will be the last one. What else can I go through? What else could I possibly learn? But then another problem arises, a bigger one, always bigger, and shows me how far I have yet to go. For every thing we learn, thousands of new lessons become visible. Like cresting a hill, only to find a mountain range beyond that, and on and on.

My foolish thoughts are about the stars. About how all that magic is there, time and creation, and I can't use it. I never knew how, and I don't know how, and no one can tell me. I wonder about the wishes—just foolishness meant to captivate a child. But what if there was something more? Who's to say? Maybe my skepticism stole it from me. Maybe my share of the magic was there and I carelessly dispersed it back to the universe. Like love, it's too late to believe after you've sent it away.

If only I could have kept believing. I don't know when I quit. But even if they didn't come true, if I had kept believing, that's where the magic was. If only I had never stopped and the magic was still there and I could look at the stars and wish and hope that it really would come true because I had never quit and the magic was only waiting until I needed it most and it was there all the time. Waiting for me to believe forever.

I don't understand it all. I don't know why some things happen, and I can't tell if it's part of the plan, or just suffering. But I'm ready to believe because I know that no one here has the answers. We're all equally lost. Except for those who believe. They have that magic. Maybe their wishes were never granted, either, but they never lost the magic. It's just waiting. Waiting for them to believe forever. And then they will be answered.

Long-term Maintenance

Schraeder came over again today with that damn chess set under his arm, and as I watched him cross the street I hoped the wind would usher him along to someone else's gate. But he entered mine, and sat opposite me at the cherry table under the wall mirror with his plastic pieces arranged neatly on an unfolded cardboard field for over twenty minutes before he came to his senses. Then he blinked as if waking from a hypnotist's trance, stared briefly into my eyes that wanted to calm him and smooth the whole thing over but only seem to speak severely lately, and with two hurried sweeps of his arm had the entire set boxed up and sprang from his chair and out the door. The gate's metallic slam punctuated his leaving like a sonic boom. He doesn't mean any harm. He's just lost his mind. And sometimes he forgets that I've lost everything else.

When the heat of afternoon subsides, Joseph, my nurse, wheels me onto the front porch, facing me toward the roses in the northwest corner of the yard one day and toward the wisteria in the northeast the next. I suppose Stella told him to do so. Well if the woman knows my wishes so well, then why not put me on the back porch so I could watch the orioles at the feeder? And why couldn't someone fix that damn windmill and stop its squealing and persistent drilling into my head. If she knows me so damn well, then why not wheel me into a closet, because she should know that watching and listening to the world that I can no longer walk through and touch and adjust and tend to is more horrible than idle minds can imagine.

The windmill, which I erected two decades ago, stands seven feet tall. With squirts of lubricant, and a few fresh coats of Rustoleum, I kept it slicing through the air smoothly for years. I stood it just this side of the iris bed, and always meant to engulf it in a brick-bordered pool of tulips. One of many things I never got around to. I suspect it wouldn't be so bad to leave this world with some trivial matters left unfinished. How could you leave it any other way? But I'm left to dwell in the midst of these unfulfilled plans with no power to tend to them.

Forty-five minutes, and it's time to go in. After cleaning me and giving me the usual speedy check-up, Joseph leaves for the night. Stella got home hours before, but has stayed in the kitchen. She began playing bridge in a club, joined the church choir, started taking walks in the morning, and has never written so many letters or spent so much time on the phone since I've known her. She doesn't love me anymore. It is not the knowledge of what has become of me that hurts. It is not even as easy as losing my hair or growing stout, but it is not what hurts. What hurts is seeing what has become of her image of me. I am a burden. Joseph does the laborious work of bathing me and lifting me in and out of bed, but it is she who must suffer my presence even when the nurse goes home.

"You don't know how small a house can be, Tina," she said on the phone once when I was within earshot. Tina is our daughter in Tucson. Juan Junior, our boy, is stationed in Germany. "At times, I can't bear to be in the same room with him. It's like waiting for a volcano to erupt, and it never does." Then a pause as Tina speaks. "No, I'm not saying that. Why would you think such a thing as that? Don't be ridiculous. I just mean I need to get out more often these days." A longer pause this time. "Well, Dear, you don't know your father like I do, and you aren't the one living here now, are you? So don't tell me how to take care of things when you're not the one in this prison."

Prison. Who is she to talk about prisons? I can't even rattle the bars of my cage to make her turn around, even though I know she's leaving me.

I can see Schraeder's silhouette through his open curtains. He lives across the street, one house up. All along the rear fence of his backyard he has a fifteen foot deep patch of rutabagas. During barbecues, or when just sitting on his back porch talking, he used to go into the plot and randomly pick one and pull it from the rich earth. Always perfect. His pride and joy. He'd rinse it at the hose spigot and slice it with a pocket knife, leaning over in his lawn chair to hand me the cut wedges. I'd dip mine in horseradish—but Schraeder would rebuke me, saying it hid the taste. "What taste?" I'd say, back when I could talk.

Prison. Before this, all I knew about prison I learned from movies. Don't think about the time, the incarcerated actors said. Don't think about those on the outside, they said. The way to make it through your sentence is to pick up something and focus on it. Either your work detail or a hobby, but something that will distract you from the clocks and calenders. Well, I surely can't whittle. Stella likes to park me in front of her game shows or just put on one of her records, as if she were making up for all the times I chose the station. But I can tune those things out when I want to. What I prefer to do to occupy the time is converse. I converse with whoever's on my mind.

"Schraeder," I say to the Schraeder who can hear me in my mind, where I am not like this, "why don't we head down to Lake Pleasant and pull out some trout this weekend?"

"Why wait for the weekend?" he says. "We're retired. Let's just go. Bring Stella and we'll make a camping trip out of it."

"Yeah, she'd really like that. You know, she used to love camping with the kids. I wish we would have done that more often."

"Hey, hey. Why so gloomy, huh?"

Oops. Reality sometimes interrupts.

After one of his lapses Schraeder mopes around the house, coming outside to trim the edges of the lawn along the walk, then sits inside his kitchen window sipping coffee, staring toward me, not knowing if I'm watching him. Every moment, buddy. Every moment I will to make him believe that there is no reason to beat himself up like that. But it takes a few days until he comes over again, even then still drenched in humiliation and self-reproach. He mumbles needless apologies as he pulls a chair up close to me. He finishes by saying, "You just don't know what it's like."

No. I don't know what it's like to wake up some mornings and not know where I am, or forget the last fifteen years of my life. But I do know what it's like to no longer be in control, and so I can't blame you for anything, Schraeder. With your body and my mind, we could be one whole man again. I need you like air.

She's the one who made it into a prison. Decades of work to pay for this house, decades of weekends spent installing new windows and siding, re-insulating the attic, remodeling the kitchen and bathrooms, putting on the new roof, building the garage, laying the driveway, planting every square inch of the yard, and God knows how many gallons of paint gone into this place, and now I am a prisoner in what was to be my castle. The stroke left me collapsed in the backyard, feeling my breath cease like the last trickle of water down a drain, the side of my face smothered in the grass, my arm pinned beneath me, there was a moment of stillness—stillness in me—when not even my heart was beating, when not even my blood pumped, like turning off your engine and headlights and coasting along a straight, deserted, pitch black length of Arizona highway on a moonless night. I was not afraid. I could have been happy to die there, oddly calm in the knowledge of what had happened. But her scream, shrill and terrified, then her hands rolling me over with strength she hadn't shown for years, threatened to break the promise of finality. Not that I had ever wished for death. No. But when it came, it was as refreshing as a glass of icy lemonade on that hot afternoon.

It wasn't only the stroke. When I collapsed, my head collided with the stone border around the garden. The synergistic effect of the two left me unable to do much more than roll my eyes. In a few seconds, I would have been free, as it was certainly intended to be. But now I'm as worthless as one of Schraeder's rutabagas. Why did she do this to me?

Now, she says she can't take it anymore. She needs a break, she says to Tina. "Tina," she says, "if you can't stay the whole week, I'm sure we can work something out with Joseph. Maybe he and one of the weekend caretakers can take shifts."

I know Tina won't hear of that.

"All right, then. You know Lorraine? She'll be here on Saturday when you get here." She pauses to listen. "Well, I had to schedule it that way. The only flight out on Saturday was at noon, so I have to take a bus to the airport in the morning. Their next flight wasn't until Monday morning."

Just can't wait to get out of here, can she?

Have you ever walked to the moon and back unaccompanied? A night can be so lonely. And so many nights I do not even blink with fatigue.

Sounds are the only motion I know now. The faint hiss of car tires slithering slowly up the asphalt on the other side of the foothills, the engine shifting lower as it nears the crest, then releasing into high gear like the first urgent breath after swimming underwater. Often you can hear their radios as they descend and breeze by the mouth of our cul de sac. I don't resent them that: it gives me something to occupy those hours. But tonight the radio voices are chopped apart by the grating, lethargic blades of the windmill. All the time moaning its rusty tenor soliloquy.

It's not a question of whether the mind will wander: It's where it may go that frightens me.

How much would I give to go hunting again just once? I don't need to shoot anything. I just need to be walking through the hills on my own two legs; my own ears hearing the frailest of twigs crisply crack; my own eyes catching the shadow-mottled hide of an elk skipping away mostly unconcerned, its tremendous mass disturbing the forest no more than a squirrel would. There are a few mounted racks and photos of me and my kills still in what was my den. Stella uses it now, but hasn't taken those things out. I wonder if it is her shrine to the man she married, who I no longer am. When she sees those photos, does her pulse still quicken, yearning for those swaggering days? Does she remember me as the man who cruised around this envious town, one hand on the wheel of his first brand new truck, one arm around her shoulder? Is it the memory of the man whose arms could lift her up, hold her tight? Does she remember when we slept in the same bed?

I can hear her breathing through the open doors between our rooms. Me in the mechanical bed, in Tina's old room, in the dark, in my mind. She in the room, in the bed, meant for us.

"Stella," I say in this attic where I am confined.

"Hmm?" she answers, as she always did, singing with curiosity.

"Why don't we go dancing tonight?"

"Dancing? Since when have you ever liked dancing?"

"Oh, you know, I've always liked dancing with you."

"You have not!" she laughs. As if wiping a foggy window, I see that we are in the garden. Every flower is in bloom. "I haven't been able to drag you out dancing for years."

"Well, then it's about time, isn't it?" I say, coming close to join my hands behind her back, pull her to me, nibble behind her right ear.

"What has gotten into you?" she giggles.

"We can dance right here," I say and start to sway my hips, drawing her along with me. I wonder if she really knew how much I enjoyed it when she "forced" me to go dancing. "Stella, honey?"

"Yes…?"

"I love you."

Schraeder. Please, I need someone to talk to. Please let this be one of your good days. Bring the old photos, bring the stories, bring the chess set if you want, but please bring yourself. Schraeder? Forty-seven cars went by between midnight and sunrise. You just have to come and talk to me. You hear me sometimes. Schraeder?

She has her bags packed, Buddy. She's leaving. She marched them right past me into the sitting room and lined them up inside the door. Each time she passes me, she tries not to look me in the eyes, but then thinks better of it and tries to reassure me with a loving glance. But it isn't love. It's pity and longing and so many emotions she has but aren't meant to be shared. Not love. Love must have dissolved as the doctors described what kind of a life I could have. When they were telling her about all the care I would need, she must have thought it only meant routine maintenance. Don't look at me like I'm a confused puppy, Stella. I need your understanding, not condescension. But how will that ever dawn upon her when I can only speak with my eyes, and I only know one language, and its only word is "hate"? I want to hate her for making me live, but I love her so much and I wish she could read my mind and then go back in time because then she would know, and she wouldn't let me stay here like this. With that grass against my cheek, and the sweat beading on my forehead no longer from toil but sweet relief, how could she not know?

Lorraine arrives with her over-sized plastic coffee mug in hand and wheels me onto the porch as casually as flipping the sign in a shop window to "Open" before the day comes to its rolling boil. She is not like Joseph. That which is a routine to Joseph is tedium to Lorraine. Clockwork. She does what needs to be done when it needs to be done, but does not understand that it is these tasks which occupy our days. She goes in to refresh her mug in our kitchen, where she will meet Stella and receive the same instructions she receives every Saturday morning as she guzzles her coffee.

Is it Lois whose white Chrysler crunches to a gradual stop in the gravel in front of our gate? I don't know the name for sure, since Stella has not introduced all of her new friends to me, but I recall her among the faces of the bridge club when they took their turn in our living room. I was already in bed for the night, so couldn't attach faces to the names they used, though I could hear every moment of their revelry. Perhaps the other women's husbands are dead. Perhaps they like it that way. Instead of coming to the door, the maybe-Lois woman taps her horn twice as if picking up a date. The image of an invalid waiting like a guard dog in front of the door you want to knock on might make anyone opt for the horn. She will drop Stella off at the bus stop. An accomplice.

Schraeder appears on his porch before Stella and Lorraine bustle out of the kitchen, push the screen open and enter my field of vision, only to continue on toward the car, where maybe-Lois pops the trunk and gets out to watch them load the bags. Then she closes the trunk as Stella comes back toward me, but continues on by and into the house. She probably left her purse in the kitchen, like always. Lorraine and Lois exchange talk about the weather over the roof of the car. Meantime, Schraeder has flown in under their radar, let himself in the unlatched gate, and proceeds to the porch, where he sits next to me on the pine bench.

"Tina's coming," Schraeder says, though I already know. He is holding my hand on my knee, which I can't feel, and wouldn't much care for if I could. "Don't you worry a bit. Tina will take care of you until Stella gets back. She's a good kid."

I hear the spring cylinder of the screen door inhale absurdly fast, then Stella is standing over me. "I'll be back soon," is all she says, as if I were a poodle. Then she hustles without running down the walk, where Lorraine closes the gate behind her.

Dammit, Stella! After all these years why can't you tell what I'm thinking? I wasn't intending to leave you, Baby. It was just such a nice invitation and everywhere I've ever worked to go. You have to understand. If it had been you. . .

"Good morning, Mr. Schraeder," Lorraine says as she reaches the steps.

"Good morning, Lorraine."

Accompanied by a single dull clunk, Lois shifts into drive, and the gravel is again hissing.

"Would you like a cup of coffee?" Lorraine asks, extending her hospitality to my kitchen.

Despite the size of her car, Lois makes a U-turn easily in the not-wide street, straightens it out, and gently brakes as she reaches the corner at the highway. I can see the back of Stella's head. Both she and Lois look left, up the hill. Though I can't see any traffic, I can hear the truck swooping down the hill, and know they're waiting for it to pass.

"Sure, that'd be fine," Schraeder says.

Then the car creeps forward. Stella looks ahead as they round the corner, points to something—maybe the flowers in someone else's yard—and talks to this Lois person as she leaves me. They accelerate out of sight behind houses, though I can hear the tires, then the engine—or maybe just an echo of them in my mind—until Lorraine reappears with Schraeder's coffee.

Morning hours trickle by.

"Daddy!" Tina exclaims as soon as she steps out of her car. She has her arms poised for a hug as she promenades up the walk, her smile so wide it's a wonder she can carry it on her wiry frame. "How are you?" she says, hugging me firmly, I suppose, but carefully, too. Even though I can't feel it, it feels good.

"Oh, I've been better," I would say.

"You know, I think I passed Mom's bus just the other side of the junction. Well, it had to be, but I couldn't see her. Anyway, it's so good to see you," she says, standing now, leaning against the railing behind her, arms folded across her stomach. "And how are you today, Mr. Schraeder?"

"Fine, fine."

I wonder if he knows who she is today.

Tina pivots my chair, takes me inside to the kitchen, where Lorraine is wiping some spilled coffee grounds across the counter and into the sink after putting on another pot. We talk about the drive down, the weather over the mountain, and whatnot. I say "we" because for once I am in the room, facing the table, and even receiving glances from Tina as if she expected me to answer. Stella gave up on talking to me long ago. I can blink for "yes" and "no," but I guess those simple questions bored her.

After this, she wheels me through the house, as if a guided tour of my own history. "Do you remember this?" she says, and tells an anecdote. "Oh, I haven't seen this for so long!" she says, though she was just here a few weeks ago.

Somehow Schraeder, who had stayed on the porch when we came inside, but later let himself in, works chess into the conversation. When Tina agrees to a game, he heads home to retrieve the set, returning to set it up on the coffee table, where he and she play, while I watch, happy to see someone finally giving him a run for his money. Lorraine is watching TV, and I wonder why we pay her. Then again, if she were fussing over me unnecessarily, I would curse her for days.

"It's about time I got to spoil you," Tina says, taking me into the back yard in the afternoon. "I guess this is how grandparents feel with their grandkids. Oh, Daddy, don't take that the wrong way. I mean, parenting probably gets tedious, day-in day-out. But to me it's a real treat getting to see you." Schraeder, who has spent most of the day with us, says, "Tina, how is it you can take a week off from school to be here?"

"Oh, it's spring break. There aren't any classes this week."

Spring break. I can't believe she's wasting her vacation time on me.

"But don't worry about it, Daddy," she says, surprising me. "I was planning to come back home, even if Mom hadn't taken her trip."

The first day is so full of action, with me as the center of every turn, until finally Lorraine has gone home, then Schraeder, and Tina is working at something I can't see from my bed. Finally, she comes into view, clears the top of the dresser, pulls out the drawers, then moves the frame to the wall in front of the foot of the bed, replaces the drawers. She's rearranging our furniture? When she leaves the room, I wonder what the living room might look like now. Has she thrown the sofa onto the lawn? But then she returns, back arced against the weight of the small TV set from Stella's bedroom. This she sets heavily on top of the dresser.

"So, what do you wanna watch?" she says. But it is not merely a rhetorical question. She produces the program guide from the newspaper, opens to today's page, and reads the show titles to me. Then she repeats the titles, one by one, watching my eyes for a response. We decide on two movies, together. "I'll be right back," she announces and disappears again. I can hear her wrestling with its ungainly weight though I can't see her through the Venetian blinds, and know even before she returns from the back patio that she will be navigating her favorite lounge chair through the hall. Onto this she plops pillows and a comforter from the hall closet. "There! All set."

We watch the comedy she chose and the classic I chose in a marathon stretch. Then she turns out the light, apparently planning to sleep right there. I'm just glad she didn't fall asleep sooner and leave me in front of the TV all night, unable to change the channel or turn the darned thing off.

"She still loves you," her voice says like an ambush from below my field of sight.

Let's just leave her out of this. She's gone and we've had the most pleasant day in months. So let's just not talk about her.

"I know you love her, too, but she thinks you hate her. She says the way you look at her makes her ashamed. Daddy, you've got to ease up on her. Nobody wanted this to happen, but just because it did doesn't mean there's someone to blame."

What can I say to that? She leaves off, her words punctuated by the stillness of night. In the subsequent absence of immediate sound the constant noises of the world fade into perception. The insects against the screens; the cars a mile away; the jingling of leaves in a sudden gust; and myriad sounds yet to be identified and cataloged by human observation. But like a hoarse voice humming without conviction, those blades scratch over it all. A needle pulled across a record. Could somebody please just oil that windmill?

"Schraeder," I say, "you're a man. You understand, don't you? Am I so hard on her, on Stella?"

"Juan, I don't want to stick my nose in." He extends a slice of rutabaga over the arm of his lawn chair. There isn't any horseradish in sight, so I wave off his offer.

"But I'm asking you to. I need to know what you think."

"Well, you two have always been a great couple, I thought."

"You thought? But what about now? You mean we aren't so good together anymore?"

"See, I don't want to get into this," he says.

"Please. If you're really my friend, you'll tell me."

"All right, then. Lately… you two just don't seem so happy. And it surprises me."

"Surprises you? Schraeder, look at me. I'm a rag doll. Is it any real shock that things have fallen apart?"

"Honestly, as your friend, yes. I've lived across the street from you for thirty years, and I never thought there were any problems in your marriage until this happened. But now I wonder what it was I wasn't seeing."

"No, you're right. There weren't any problems until this. I tell you, we were in love every day of our lives."

"Well, if that's true, then how could you have fallen out of love so quickly? Yeah, yeah, I know about the stroke. But what if you had died? If you had died, do you think she would have stopped loving you? Do you really think her love is attached to your body, and not your soul?"

The problem with performing these scenes in one's mind is that in the absence of real interlocutors Abstraction and Philosophy read all the good lines.

Aside from the odd sensation of waking up in anticipation of the day, Sunday morning holds a wonderful surprise. By the time Lorraine and Tina have me out on the front porch, Schraeder is already in our front lawn, tool box by his feet, craning over the propeller of the windmill.

" I hope you don't mind, Buddy," he says, "but I figured someone should grease this thing."

God bless you!

Schraeder pauses like an animal when a person approaches, looks at me, squints as if to recognize me, and I fear he has had a lapse. But then he smiles and says, "Well, you're welcome, Buddy."

This was not all in my mind.

I'm giddy like a toddler with a growing vocabulary, hoping for a chance to demonstrate my skills. In the last months, I haven't felt anything remotely like enthusiasm, and now here it is, swathed in enough energy I think I can walk again, wave my arms, tap my foot, nod my head. Mountainous aspirations. I must be changing, my shell melting from all this radiation. I wish I could smile.

Did I say so much with my eyes? Or was it that Schraeder finally looked close enough to see how I feel? But how could I ever convince Stella to look me in the eye, to linger there, to peer hard enough to see my mind? My heart.

"Honey," I want to say, "we've got to work together. Let's not talk about what happened, or if we had it all to do over again. Let's just go forward. I don't want to be angry, or hurt, and I don't want to injure you anymore."

It's funny how one day ago I thought her leaving would kill me. Maybe it did. Maybe without someone to be angry at, the angry me did die. Maybe it was never her I was angry at, but myself. Infuriated to be shown pity. Frustrated that what I saw in the way she looked at me was true. There is sorrow here. There is shame. There is anger and remorse and a colossal burden of heartbreak. But these are not because of the stroke and the fall. These are because her eyes have been mirrors of my own, and I was the one who suffocated the love.

Those days go by so quickly, but with so much progress. It hasn't come back, that sinister side of me. When Stella returns, will the situation revert to the way it was? Will I start to hate myself again? Or will she be ready to accept that I have changed? Just a few days ago, when someone would look into my eyes, I would stare ahead without blinking, as if someone were knocking on my front door and I were remaining perfectly still to suggest that no one were home. Playing opossum. It was my last defense.

Here is how much I have accomplished: Today I am sitting on the back porch, watching the orioles feed from a fresh bag of seed poured into the feeder. Yes! Now that people are not afraid to look into my eyes, we can communicate again. To a limited degree, of course, but after months of life like a wooden Indian, this is as refreshing as an evening by the sea.

"First dancing, and now this?" she says, seated at our single table overlooking the white sands in the moonlight. "What's next? A picnic in a Swiss meadow?"

"Maybe so. I don't know what we'll do next. I just want to make every moment with you as lovely as you have been to me all these years. I know I can't erase all the times I've been gruff and stubborn, but if we make more good memories, maybe those will be what come to mind when you think of us."

I think of things to say to her. Limited as I am, I only hope she grasps the extent of my effort. If I were still able to talk and move around like a king, how easy it would be to woo her: how less moving the same words might be.

We are watching TV in the living room, Tina and I. The hardest part about watching game shows is not being able to say the answers out loud. The rattling sounds of Lorraine checking my equipment in my room don't drown out the show. Sunday evening once again. Stella will be home any time now. Her flight should have landed a while ago, and she should be on the bus. Stella, I can imagine how you feel, coming back to this prison after being free for a week, but you're going to be surprised. I really have changed.

"You knew that one, didn't you, Daddy?" Tina says, patronizing me to just the right measure.

Commercials are an exercise in patience when you can not change channels or bolt to the kitchen for a quick snack.

And now the news, which means she should just be getting into town. Then that Lois—it'll take some time to extend my newfound kindness to everyone—will pick her up and she should be home before the sports report. Will she see it in my eyes as soon as she opens the door? I feel like she has to, like I am the cutest puppy, wagging its tail, and who can resist these big, brown eyes?

Special Report? Well, that depends on your—Is that our airport? What's she saying? I can't hear with all the clamor in the background. The line at the bottom of the screen says it's our airport. Live.

Tina deflates with an ascending "O-o-ohhhhhh!" which never peaks, but transforms into a dry, squeaking, stuttering sob. Though I can't see her face, I know it is collapsed upon itself with grief, the way my heart has just shriveled into a raisin.

When Lois arrives to tell us that Stella wasn't on the bus and did she change her plans, Tina's face is pink from crying, but she has calmed her sobs and has finally reached the airline on the phone, but is still unable to get any kind of confirmation. Staring blankly at the cable news channel with its continuing coverage of the crash, its repeated use of "killed instantly," I am trying to find something to say.

Reservations

"Are you sure you're ready for this?" he asked.

Outside the comfortable dome of the car, the sudden assemblage of buildings seemed simultaneously reminiscent of a ghost town and eastern city slums. "I think so," she said.

Holbrook, Arizona mirrors a white person's concept of destitution. At least until they see the reservation. Route 66 used to course through Holbrook's heart, parading hundreds of open-road-spendthrift Easterners by the shops full of moccasins and rabbit foot key-chains, "Made by REAL Indians!" The bulk of the U.S. population lived east of here, and everyone wanted to see the Grand Canyon, which lies west, so they made their way through Holbrook. Until the interstate. Now the pitch of their radials grows lower as they decelerate down the off-ramp, followed by the averting of their eyes as they turn onto Navajo Boulevard and pass Navajo and Hopi bag-ladies, toothless under the bandannas that failed some years ago to protect their minds from the broiling heat, waddling in such unmistakable pain that any podiatrist would whimper with sympathy. While they wait for their order at Burger King—letting the kids run up the street to Taco Bell—they take turns using the restrooms, then zip back onto I-40 without ever seeing the rows of novelty motels, one of which is cabin-style, with all the rooms shaped like tipi's, except the air-conditioners plugged into the rectangular windows. Elsewhere above the painted earth, Fred Harvey's name adorns visitor centers and shuttle buses as if this had always been his land.

Petrified wood. Petrified progress.

There's a bar near the railway crossing, near that famous petrified wood store with the huge dinosaurs out front, where he has never seen less than two Hopi men seated on the sidewalk, defeated. Navajo or Hopi. But saying Hopi hurts less. Local newspapers loved to tell of the hostility between Navajos and Hopis back in 1992 when the white voters of Arizona were deciding how to once again apportion the land where others lived. They really talk up those ancient land feuds. But, looking through the tinted window of his Stratus Coupe, he doesn't feel a need to hate anyone. Air conditioning and a good sound system can absolve tremendous grudges.

Still, if white people want to talk about land feuds…

His father never had reason to go farther than Gallup, New Mexico, and never fabricated one, either. Beyond the four corners, the whole wide world was equivalent to static from outer space making the television reception snowy. And his father never watched television. Sheep rancher. A man who enjoyed ranching sheep.

But the boy resisted. Studied hard in the schools staffed by white teachers "doing their time" on the reservation, teaching how to adapt to the white world, as if that were what everyone should want to do. Those teachers—most of whom bolted for good as soon as they landed a better job—never would understand why Indians, as people will always persist in calling them, would seem to succeed in high school, move to Holbrook or Winslow to attend Northland Pioneer Community College, and be back on the reservation with an Associates degree in their pocket. No one really needed an Associates degree on the reservation.

A red Dodge Stratus Coupe. Impenetrable black tinting on all the windows. Not coated from the bottom up with red clay like every vehicle on the reservation.

"That's where I used to work," Thomas said, lifting his right hand just above the steering wheel to indicate the Basha's supermarket. "Studied over at the junior college for two years and lived in a motel room with the money from the supermarket. My first job."

Glancing at the intermittent pedestrians, all of them short and dark-skinned, Amber wondered how many Native Americans she had seen in her life. Just one, she had thought. The rest were Mexican, right? But now she saw that she wasn't sure. No one from Des Moines thinks much about Native Americans, except the notion that they all live in the Southwest.

Her skin was fair, even for a white girl. Natural blond hair, curled inward slightly to frame her neck. Her name, too, was blond: Amber. If only she had come from a more sophisticated city, like Chicago, or Pittsburgh.

But beggars can't be choosers, especially Navajo beggars in Arizona bars. It is illegal for women to even glance at "Indian" men romantically. "Indian" men aren't there for the social scene: they're there to drink. Don't they know they could have saved some money by going to 7-11?

But Amber had not been in Tempe long enough to be thoroughly educated. She had been hired as an accountant for an IT firm, which were sprouting all around, as Phoenix was tons cheaper than San Jose. Anyhow, maybe she was intrigued, or maybe she thought he was a Mexican—women are allowed to get tangled up with Mexicans, as long as they are at least second generation and are more fluent in English than Spanish. Either way, he never hunched over his beer in shame or self-pity, no matter how the Natives (of Tempe, that is) winced at the thought of having him in their lounge, so his eyes were scanning the room and happened upon hers. The reason she had wanted to come talk to him may even have been because she thought neither one of them belonged. She could hardly carry on a conversation with Tempe Natives, because she didn't know about the Sun Devils, didn't know about the Rio Salado Canal, didn't know about the vortex in Sedona or the Granolas in Flagstaff. She didn't know that Begay and Yazzie were Navajo names as common as Smith or Jones in her own white pages back home. She expected Whitecloud or Manyhorses. All she really knew about Arizona was that by mid-April the sun could wither your skin like shrink-wrap.

And so they met.

Pulled up under the shade of the white concrete wall of the gas station after filling the tank, he said, "We're about an hour away now. I was thinking maybe we ought to get a room back at the Holiday Inn Express. We could drive out there tonight, come back to sleep, then go out in the morning again."

He sounded quite unsure of his plan. "Whatever you think is best," she said.

He seemed to be thinking for a moment, though she could tell he wasn't actually calculating distances.

"Well, I guess we can just go on out there. If we have to, I'd bet there'll be an open room somewhere. There's like a thousand motel rooms in town."

Eleven hundred and forty, she corrected him in her mind. She had looked up the Chamber of Commerce web site to preview their weekend getaway, as she mistakenly romanticized it. He had said it was to meet the family, and he had repeatedly beseeched her not to expect too much, but how could someone from Des Moines imagine what she would soon see? Hogans, for she didn't know what else to call them, made of mud and branches, atop rolling hills of the most uncultivable, inhospitable landscape (she couldn't even call it "land") imaginable. No, worse than imaginable. No one could imagine this until they had witnessed it.

"Those aren't the houses," he explained about the hogans, catching her staring as he drove. "Those are mostly just for sheep herders to stay in when they're with their flocks."

When they turned west from Dilkon, she felt some satisfaction that she had finally seen what passed for a reasonable settlement. Still, the homes and stores were all like military base homes, erected in neat patterns of cheap materials and simple designs.

Soon they pulled into a driveway which seemed to service a small cluster of assorted trailers and a few mobile homes arranged around one permanent dwelling, slightly sturdier than the ones in Dilkon. The high tailgates of full-sized trucks boasted "Chevrolet" through their clay overcoats. Somehow this gave the impression of a herd of horses drinking from a central pool. It was not yet too late to pull the shifter back into "reverse" and chuckle, telling her it was all a joke. No one had yet emerged from the pull-behind trailer or pressed their face to the sagging screen of the house's front door to see who had pulled up. Then, with a crisp peeling sensation, the hopeful air evacuated as the sedimentary air of "the Rez" rushed through her open door. Her right foot was already on the ground.

Thomas had no choice but to turn off the ignition and arise from the car as she was standing in the space between car and open door, and he could see a large figure pausing just inside the screen door to assess who the visitors might be, then pull a red t-shirt over his head. Thomas stepped into the heat and dizzying sun, closed the door just as the door on the house sprung open and not one, but two men slightly larger than he sauntered out.

"Ya'at'eeh, cousin!" the one in the red t-shirt called, thumbs in his belt loops, jerking his chin up and head back in salute, as men do.

"Hey, cousin," Thomas said, reciprocating none of the long-time-no-see affection. "Speak English, huh?"

"Me no speakum English," the same one said, deepening his voice to mimic the kind of Greek actors who masqueraded as "Injuns" in old Monument Valley westerns.

"Well," the one behind him said, "I speak rather delightful English." He seemed to be aspiring toward a British accent, but arrived somewhere closer to a Frankenstein imitation.

"Knock it off," Thomas said, leading her toward them. "This is Amber."

"Hey," the first one said.

"Hey," the other echoed.

"Amber, this is my cousin, Charles —"

"Chuck," he corrected.

"— and my little brother, Lucas."

"Nice to meet you. Thomas has told me a lot about you."

Chuck guffawed. "Yeah?"

"Is Mom home?" Thomas said, inviting himself out of the sun.

"Yeah, she's sleeping," Lucas said, holding the door open.

Inside the house, Amber was faintly disappointed to find Art Barn prints hung over the Ethan Allen furniture and Pier 1 Imports accents. But it was cool, even without a fan, and they sat together facing the TV, which was tuned to a figure skating exhibition performance.

"When'd you get the TV?" was the first thing Thomas asked.

"Been in here for more'n a year," Lucas said. "Had it out in the trailer 'til Pop died. He didn't like so much noise," he added in Amber's direction.

"Hey," Chuck said like a burp. "Whatchu doing tonight? Wanna come on inna Holbrook and watch the dances with us?"

"What time are you heading in?" Thomas asked.

"Leave here about five," he said.

"What dances?" Amber asked, intending to be part of the conversation, even if left out of the decision.

"Indian dances," Chuck said. "They have them outside the old courthouse all summer."

Indian dances. Ironic that they would have to leave the reservation to see authentic Indian dances, Amber mused.

"If we'd have known, we could have just waited down there for you. Could have saved us a trip," Thomas said. Could have saved me the embarrassment, he thought. He looked at his watch. "It's almost four, now."

"We're gonna spend the night in town," Chuck said.

Thomas knew what that meant: they were planning to drink a lot. It also most likely indicated that his mother would not be joining them, as she rarely slept away from her own bed.

"I'm gonna go wake up Mom," Thomas said.

The old woman's appearance entertained Amber's fancy of what Native Americans should look like: hair back in double braids, box dress, wise pebbles for eyes. She preceded Thomas's re-appearance through the narrow hallway, talking to him, though looking straight ahead until her eyes locked on Amber, at which point her head turned like a rudder, though the body drifted a few steps atop its own momentum before responding and turning toward the couch. She stood just beyond the arm of the couch, short and small-boned, looking somehow like she were the child seeking approval.

"Amber, this is my mom. Mom, this is Amber," Thomas said, a few steps behind.

Amber stood, wondered if she should extend her hand, but that was a man's greeting, so just said, "It's very nice to finally meet you."

But the old woman blinked and turned her head toward the TV, moved to sit in a chair against the wall. "She's pretty, Thomas. So what's next?"

"What?" Thomas said, standing over the back of the sofa, placing a hand on Amber's shoulder to comfort her, though she showed no signs of needing it. She, in fact, wished to re-seat herself, but remained standing to let her shoulder support Thomas.

"Didn't you bring us anything else?" she said.

"He got a new car," Chuck tattled.

"Another new one?" The last time he had come back, he drove a Chevy Blazer with a leather interior and less than twenty thousand miles on it, and refused to let Chuck try out the four wheel drive. "Well, has he shown it to you yet?"

"Nope," Chuck said, playing the accomplice to her impassivity, though a hint of mirth attended his voice.

"Thomas," she said, "why haven't you shown off your new car yet?"

"Ma..."

"No, Thomas. We all know what you came here for. Now get to it."

The three of them banished out the front door, Amber sat back down on the couch. Thomas's mother ignored her without effort.

"Thomas talks about you often," Amber said with little hope of it breaking the ice. Even if she didn't know the particulars it didn't take a psychologist to observe the turbid family dynamics at play.

The old woman snorted. "All about his wonderful family?"

Amber tread cautiously, stopping to consider her answer. Honestly, he did not lavish compliments toward his mother, except as apologia for his other remarks. When the old woman heard no response forthcoming, she shot a quick glance in Amber's direction, snorted again, then resumed watching TV.

"What's she talking about?" Thomas said.

"Never mind. Just pop the hood, eh? What's she got? Six cylinder?"

Thomas ducked inside the door to release the hood. "What? Yeah. Six cylinder. Two point five liter."

"How fast does it go?" Lucas said.

"Who cares? How many horse trailers can you pull uphill with it. That's important," Chuck taunted.

"There's no trailer hitch," Thomas said, oblivious to the sarcasm in his cousin's voice. "What's she mean, you know what I came here for? I came here to visit. That's all."

"And to introduce us to your new girlfriend," Chuck reminded.

"Yeah, of course. I don't get it. Why's she mad at me?"

Chuck sighed, enjoying Thomas's bewilderment act because Thomas probably had no idea that he was acting. "So, cousin, you gonna let me drive this to Holbrook?"

Chuck drove Lucas in his Chevy, tailgating the Stratus for the merriment of watching Thomas monitor the rear-view mirror, and periodically tap the brake lights to make them ease off. Amber scanned the alien landscape out her window.

"So, where do you want to stay… back in town?" Thomas asked.

"Wherever. You know better than me."

" I guess maybe we should go to the Holiday Inn, then," Thomas said, clearly requesting affirmation.

"Anywhere's fine."

Thomas had never been to the Holiday Inn Express. He had been to better hotels when he traveled for conventions over the past few years, but there was a mystique about the one particular hotel in the one town that he never stayed in. He didn't know anyone who had. Which is not to suggest that the hotel refused Navajo patrons, but maybe that Navajo patrons saw no need to stay there when there were cheaper motels along every street.

"I don't know," Thomas said. "I mean, they'll probably get pretty drunk. Maybe we should go some place where they won't get themselves into any trouble."

Hands at ten and two o'clock, Thomas considered several schemes in which he could drop Chuck and Lucas off at some dark motel and take Amber to a suite at the Inn. Not that he would mind paying for them to stay in the Inn, too, but the experience would not be the same with two drunk Navajos in tow. The core of the fantasy was not to defy the establishment.

"I wish he'd quit that," Thomas snapped. Amber shifted her hips, looked around. Chuck swiped a "Hi" sign with the single hand near the crest of the steering wheel, easing the truck back as he did. She knew Chuck was just kidding around, but also knew better than to say it. Still, Thomas seemed to sense this.

"He ought to be more careful," he said in his own defense. "More Indians die on these roads...drunk drivers, mostly."

"Well, he hasn't been drinking, yet," Amber said playfully, deciding both to join the argument he was intent on pursuing, and also trying to add some levity.

"Still, these Indians just don't seem to know how to drive, sometimes," Thomas said.

Safe on the cooling pavement of Holbrook, the four of them walked a few blocks from their parking places toward the courthouse, stopping at a gas station to buy bottled water and beer.

"Don't worry, cousin," Chuck said as he caught Thomas staring at the six-pack he put on the counter. "We'll take it easy. Right, Lucas?"

"Mmm," Lucas asserted.

Amber had remained outside to browse the silver and turquoise jewelry in an adjacent window. Rejoining them, walked side-by-side behind the others, until they jaywalked across the street. Only through the way he held her hand, Thomas urged her to continue until the crosswalk.

Chuck and Lucas grabbed a good spot with room in front of them for Thomas and Amber. The dances had already begun, but it was just some kids, getting practice before the not-yet capacity crowd. Here and there, near the parked cars or on the edge of the gathering, circulating crowd, Amber could see men in bright headdresses and beads, whose posture did not suggest that of a dancer.

They were not stretching. But when the floodlights became necessary under the dimming sky and the adorned men took their positions, they stamped and spun, bowed and arced with an indefatigable pride which mocked the rehearsed care which stifles the most famed dancers. Later on, the announcer would invite the spectators to join in the dance, and a few dozen like-spirited souls would trample the ground in chaotic unison, all to the same drum and singer. When this time came, Chuck and Lucas eagerly sprung up from their haunches, danced alone, circled back to find each other, met women who they soon lost again in the massive swirl comprised of local eddies. But Thomas, for all Amber's pleas, resisted, finally pulling his hand from hers, leaving her to stand over him for a moment before turning to find Lucas, shadow him around the congregation. As the song neared its end, Thomas stood, brushed off his pants, and waited for Amber to come around like she was an open spot on a merry-go-round. Before she reached him, though, the song ended abruptly, the windmill made of human pinwheels sputtering to a stop.

"Oh, I was just coming to join you," Thomas said.

"Ah, bull!" Chuck said, coming up from behind him, brow beaded with sweat. "Thomas don't like to dance like a Injun."

But Thomas wouldn't let himself be boxed in. "So, you guys ready for some dinner? I'm buying."

"Of course you're buying," Chuck said, turning his head to watch a short-ish young woman in Wrangler jeans walk by.

"So, what do you want?" Thomas said to Amber.

"I don't know. What's good around here, Luke?" she said, trying on the abbreviated name, which the others excused.

"Uh, the Taco Bell?" Lucas proposed.

"No. No Taco Bell. She lives in Tempe. She can have Mexican beans any time. What she's up here for is a cultural exchange. Right, Thomas?" Chuck said. Then directing himself to Amber, "You ever try Navajo Tacos?"

"Navajo Tacos?" Amber said.

"Yeah. You'll love 'em. They got beans and lettuce and peppers on fry bread. Really good."

"But we can go to that... what's the name of that place up there near the KOA? We can up to that steak house," Thomas said, adding "If you want" as an afterthought.

"No. The Navajo Tacos sound good. I like to try new things," she said, canceling his protestations with the efficiency of hanging a bounced check in a gas station window.

Chuck led them up Navajo Boulevard, turning off the street with no curb where a van was parked alongside the road, sliding door agape, an awning stretching from the van to cover the small set-up where a short woman with braids past her belt was selling drinks from an orange Gatorade cooler, and frying up Navajo Tacos on a gas-powered stove. Amber and Thomas sat on the tailgate, Chuck and Lucas above them on the sides of the truck bed, eating the tacos from flimsy paper plates across the tops of their thighs, watching the cars zip by, stars come out.

Chuck said with an air of conclusion, "This is a Navajo evening."

Thomas considered how true that might be. But where were the stumbling drunk natives? Chuck and Lucas had held true to their word, and were only on their third beers in so many hours. Didn't all Indians drink all the time? Wasn't that how he remembered it? And when had he sat on a tailgate eating Navajo Tacos? More like a hillside, watching sheep while his father got some dinner. Still, the sky had not changed. The silent weeping of the stars, appearing one-by-one like luminescent tears dripping from above this azure dome, could never have been wiped away from memory.

"Charming," Amber said. "I could get used to this."

Thomas could count the illuminated windows in the Holiday Inn Express. What would they think? Three Navajo men, smelling of beer and dried sweat, escorting a single white female up to the desk?

"Hey, didn't I see a Dairy Queen by the overpass," Amber asked.

"Yeah," Lucas blurted, as if the first word following a vow of silence.

"What do you guys want? My treat," she said. "Dilly Bars? Peanut Buster Parfait?"

She took their orders and she and Lucas drove the coupe away from Thomas and Chuck still on the tailgate in the sandy gravel alongside the road. Thomas regretted letting them go alone, sensing a missed opportunity to swing through the Basha's parking lot to give her a closer look of his old stomping grounds. And why had they waited here for the others to bring the ice cream? Because people waited here, Chuck would tell him, and he would be right. People were always pulled off the road, vehicles forming a "V," talking or drinking.

"If you ever get tired a that one, let me know," Chuck said. "I'll take 'er off your hands."

"I just got 'er a few months ago. I don't think I'll be trading that one in for a few years," Thomas said.

"Not the car."

Thomas turned toward him without revealing his indignation. "What did you say?"

"Amber. Now that everyone has seen her and knows that you got yourself a good white woman, I guess you can throw her away, huh?"

"What are talking about? How drunk are you?"

"I ain't drunk, Cousin. You still actin' like you don't know. Why your ma is mad at you. She's mad you broke up with Tina."

"Tina? Mom hated Tina. You all hated her."

"No, we didn't. Your ma thought she was real nice. You know, they had a good long talk without you that weekend. Yeah, your ma really took to her."

"This is ridiculous. I remember. Everyone was so uncomfortable around her. That's why I broke up with her."

While Chuck turned his head to spit over the wall of the truck bed, Thomas checked the road to see if the others were on their way back yet.

"Why you always the only one don't know what yer doin'?" Chuck asked.

"What? You're going to have to share your superior wisdom with me, man."

"You broke up with Tina because we liked her. It was you making everyone uncomfortable. You didn't want us to like her. You go out and bring back your white world to the reservation and you think we should be disappointed. We're not. We're proud of you. You know, most of the people who say they never want to leave the reservation, they already tried. They got to say that now."

Thomas smiled, looked up at the stars, shook his head slowly. "Let me make sure I've got this right. You mean I don't want you to approve of me?"

"Yeah. That's the third new car you've shown up with in five years, ain't it?"

"So?"

"So, take a look at yourself, Cousin. You brought Amber up here to show us how successful you are, and now you're going to break up with her to punish yourself for not being Navajo enough."

"I know you're not drunk, so you must be nuts. Is there some quiz in the *Navajo Times* to see if you're an apple or not? Is that it? Well, don't bother with the psycho-analysis. If I need help in that department—"

"—You'll go to a white doctor. Yeah, I know."

Amber's Blizzard had Reese Peanut Butter Cups and a banana chopped up and swirled together. She let each of them taste it, though they each shriveled their noses as if taking cough medicine before doing so, underwriting the prospect of not liking the combination. Lucas was the first to complain of an ice cream headache.

Break up with Amber? If only he knew. They had come up to announce their engagement. Break up with her? She was incomparable. And as for giving a damn about what these people thought about him, well, Chuck had better think again about all that nonsense. He had broken up with Tina because… Oh, what difference does it make, why he did it? It had just become necessary. They had reached a point where there was no more growing together to be done. That it coincided with taking her home to meet the family was meaningless. No, wait. He remembered why. Yeah, that's right, the way she started acting. She started acting like he was dirty. She saw his family, and she could never think of him as anything but some Navajo refugee from the rez after that. That's right. That's how it happened. The family didn't like her, and she didn't like them, and Thomas wasn't able to please either side, much less both. And, yeah, it just might happen again. Look at them, drinking beer in the back of a truck. How could she like them?

"This reminds me of being back in Iowa with my brothers," Amber said, as if to counter Thomas's reasoning. "I have two older brothers. Danny and Kyle. We used to sit in Danny's Ford up on this hill above the river in the summers. Just drinking and talking, or sitting quietly. Maybe go down for a dip if some friends pulled in next to us."

None of the men could imagine clearly what it would be like to have a plush river running nearby, but tried, nonetheless, enchanted by her desire to remember. She had a voice like a river, Thomas thought, but thought it might not be, because rivers could be loud. He had seen a few rivers. Anyway, it was a voice you could close your eyes and listen to. Steady and uncomplaining. Gently adamant.

"Got any more of them beers?" Amber asked to the guys behind her.

"Nope. All out. Guess it's time to go to bed," Chuck said.

"What? What time is it? It can't be past ten."

"Ten-thirty, almost," Lucas said.

"What, are you getting up early for church? You're not tired, too, are you, Thomas?"

Thomas looked at his watch, though he knew he had just heard Lucas say what time it was. “Well, I guess it isn’t that late. You wanna head over to Basha's and pick up a twelve pack?”

Chuck perked his ears. “You talkin’ to me?”

“Yeah. A twelve pack. Or two six packs. Whatever. I want Bud Ice. What do you want?”

“Bud Ice is fine. You feelin’ all right, Cousin?”

“Yeah, yeah. Hey, you guys ever stay in the Holiday Inn Express?” Thomas asked.

“Oh, yeah, all the time.”

“Good. You guys go get the beer, and we’ll go get a room before they’re full. Meet you back here?”

“That good with you, Amber?” Chuck asked, deferring to the guest.

“Sure.”

“Hey, you know where’d be good?” Lucas said. “The flats out there by the Woodruff turn-off. That’s quiet.”

“Yeah. That is real, real quiet.”

Room keys in the glove box, Thomas drove behind the Chevy the seven miles to the turn off. Better not drink more than a few. We can come back in the morning to get the pickup, if the boys get carried away. But someone needs to drive. Besides, what would the point be of going to the Inn if you pass out as soon as you get there. No, better just get a buzz on under the stars. Later, I can be the first Navajo I know to get drunk in the Holiday Inn Express. First one to wake up there with his hung-over family.

Exhale

Between the blinks of the Christmas lights wrapped around my windows, an intermittent astronomy flashes above me. Lights on, stars off. Lights off, stars on. Peaceful. Almost enough to distract my fear.

December. Pretty late in the year for there not to be snow. One-thirty. Pretty late at night for me to be sprawled on my back on my front lawn with only a pair of boxer shorts and my robe on. But don't worry: the neighbors are all asleep. Besides, they already know I'm weird. They've seen me piss on the tree in my backyard during a summer barbecue instead of going inside because I was drunk. They've seen me in the driveway, working on my hobby car, talking to it, promising it a new set of spark plugs if the clutch would just work right. They don't seem to care what I do as long as I don't talk to them.

My sister is in the hospital. She was pregnant, but that's not exactly why she's in there. She's in there because of Dirk. Her own husband. I'd kill him if I was back east. I'd break both of his arms and smash his kneecaps with a bat and hold him up by his tender throat and say to him, Why the hell'd you hurt my sister? and he'd be crying, looking in my eyes which would never let him live, and he'd say some crap about he was sorry and didn't mean it and Please, man, don't hurt me! but I'd be shaking with rage and he hurt my sister and I would kill him.

She might lose her baby.

Shooting star. It made a streak all the way across Orion's shoulders. Orion's above me. Legs spread and arms over his head, just like me, projected into the universe. Transposed. Or maybe I'm him focused on the ground. Doesn't matter. There's one up there and one down here, and we never talk anyway.

I have my cordless phone right next to me. I could call him and say, Hey, Orion, Baby! Long time no see, man. Let's get together, have a few beers, shoot some pool, shoot the shit. But I think maybe he's got caller I.D. and doesn't want to talk to me. He knows how I spend my Sundays, playing pool or fishing or laying in bed with my girlfriend until early afternoon, and he decides he ain't got time for my kind, you know. Fine by me. I ain't got time for him, either.

Besides, the phone's so Mom can call.

He jumped right on her. She's eight months pregnant and cleaning his house and doing his dishes, and it ain't enough for him. He needs to be a man. Needs to show he's tough. So he slaps her around. He slaps my sister, and maybe belts her with his knuckles, too, and he pushes her and knocks her around and then when she's on the floor crying because he's such a bastard he jumps right on her stomach, right on her baby, right on his own son.

If it wouldn't have been so late, and I could have got a ticket, I'd be on a plane and me and Dirk would be talking soon.

But someone needs to talk to my sister, too, Orion. Someone needs to remind her that she got straight A's in high school, and that she was doing fine in the junior college before this prick showed up, and that she's wonderful—because she is. Someone needs to give her back her self respect. Right now, though, someone just needs to let her keep her baby.

There's that phone next to me, and I think maybe I could call him and he would answer and he could let her keep the baby. And I wouldn't mind calling, either, except I'm afraid of maybe blowing her chances because I'm not the right person to be calling and asking.

Once, I was snorkeling, and I decided to lay on my back on the bottom of the sea, and I pulled off my snorkel, then exhaled, and the air bubbles rising through the water looked just like my breath rising above me now. Only now it's slower. Now it doesn't want to leave me so desperately. Now isn't as frivolous, like looking up from the bottom of a glass of champagne.

Inside my house, there's a fire in the wood-burning stove. The smoke rises from the chimney like my breath from me. Cautiously, slowly, like it's making sure no one needs it before it leaves.

The Christmas lights keep winking. Quiet. All that motion of red, green, yellow, orange, blue—and nothing but stillness. Nothing distant, nothing close, nothing moving, nothing alive.

Quiet. No neighbors, no cars, no airplanes, no television, not even me. Quiet.

No phone ring, either.

I probably won't fly out there. I want to. There's a something in me that tastes like blood and is ready to erupt and is restless, anxious, restless. But to let it loose would just make things worse. My sister needs her rest, and everything needs to settle, and she couldn't bear me killing someone—and I really would kill him. Or at least want to.

No, that wouldn't help any. So I'll leave it to you to take care of him. But first, couldn't you take care of Sis?

They're taking the baby out because it isn't breathing right. Mom made it sound a little trickier than a normal operation because they've got to watch the breathing and all. Not breathing, really, but—what do you call it—respiration!—the lungs. Can hardly breath when you're inside someone. Can hardly breath when Orion's above you and the phone won't ring, and maybe he's sitting on the edge of his cloud, waiting for my call. Distraught. Just like me. Why don't you pick up the phone?

No moon, either. It's vacationing over Lebanon right now.

I should maybe go inside. The Christmas lights blink an eerie but warm Morse code invitation for me to put my feet in front of the fire, have a sip of hot chocolate—with just a touch of butterscotch schnapps—watch the news channel and see how the Bears did today. I should go in before I'm paralyzed out here. Numb.

But I can't. It's like… it's like a staring contest. I can't take my eyes off him. He's watching me, too. One of us has to give in.

It's the dumbest thing, and I haven't thought of it for years, but now it's stuck in my head. When I was nine and she was six, we were in the backyard one day and I took her favorite doll away from her. She cried and bawled and I kept teasing her, laughing. I was taller and she couldn't reach as I held the doll above my head. She calmed down and asked me politely if she could have her doll back. I considered it. She had surrendered. I had won. I should have given it back. Instead, I pulled its stupid arm off and waved it in front of my sister's face. She shrieked and whirled around and ran inside to tell while I hid behind a tree and tried to put that damned arm back on, but I had ruined it.

When Mom came out, I got a few swats—but Mom's swats never hurt. And then she told me I had to pay for a new doll out of my allowance. But my sister wouldn't let me. It wasn't a doll, she kept saying as she cried. It was her baby. Hell, I never knew she loved her toys like that. I felt like dirt for a long time.

Well, Dirk, how about you? Do *you* feel like dirt? How about it, Dirk… you gonna buy her a new baby now?

You must have a good view from up there. How many eyes does it take, I used to wonder, to watch all of our minute lives? And how could you keep track of it all? So I guess it must be me reflecting you down here, because I can't even imagine the answers to these questions. But, you know, when you're a kid you just forget—or never knew or couldn't understand in the first place—that a half dozen billion other people are living on this planet, and you figure yours is the only life being watched. Being really watched. Every thing you do, even when you're in the room with your door shut, being quiet so your parents can't hear, even then, you recall that someone's got a bird's eye view.

It must be nice.

That's what I thought. I thought it must be nice to see Amy Peterson get undressed at night. I thought you got to see all the good stuff. And then I was suddenly twenty-two, and I figured out, without having thought about it for years, that that's not what you see. Your vision is different, in ways I don't understand. Our hearts are what you see. So I looked inside my own heart to share the view, but it was like looking at a national park forest burned and littered. Not a blossom anywhere. Not a sapling of hope. I thought, Jesus, how am I gonna ever restore all that? And I am still so ashamed that I've just closed the park down.

Slowly, now. The world turns slowly. Breath drifts away like an evaporating wish. Dissipates. Disappears. Grey mist hope and crisp air reality. Shaken, not stirred. Slowly, slowly. Cautious, calm.

I'd offer you a beer, but you're already exalted. What can I get you? What can I do for you? Isn't there something? Listen, I'll make you a deal. I could quit hating if you would give in. How about it? Talk to me, and I'll never swear again. Come on. It can't be that tough. Just wave at me, wink at me, blow me a kiss, and I'll do nothing but love for all my life. Send me a letter, visit me, let me know you know my name, and I'll praise you forever.

Please? Just stop being so silent. Can you hear me? Please.

Save my sister's baby, and I'll give in. You can win again. You can stay quiet and hidden and never drop a line. It's all right. You can love me or leave me or laugh in my face. All right? I never meant to disappoint you, and if I had known then how all your time is spent watching your loved ones fail I would've done everything I could to have saved you the added disappointment of my mistakes. I would have tried to have made you proud, just like a father.

See this? See my face? I can feel tears running toward my ears, wanting to freeze. And I've started shaking. I've been out here for over an hour, and only now I'm shaking. Come on! What do you want?

...No answer.

The phone sleeps next to me annoyingly. It's like when you're awake in the middle of the night and you're wife's asleep and you want to "accidentally" wake her up so you have someone to talk to. Doesn't work with phones, though. They wake up when they want to. Like babies.

My fire is dying. My chimney is out of breath. The last wraith of smoke floats toward a star ten thousand light years above me to tell it that I'm down here waiting. By then it might be a little too late.

Something in me wants to believe. Did you know that? Something tells me that since I'm talking to you I do believe. And I want to ask you every five seconds to make the phone ring and let me hear that everything's all right so that when it does ring I will have just asked you and then I can say that you did it. See? I want to believe. Really. But I can't.

I don't know if it's because I work everyday for what I have and I don't want to admit that I should be spending more time looking after my soul instead, or if it's because I've done so much that's wrong that if I did believe it would mean I'd have to be guilty, or what. I don't know if maybe it's because you can't love me.

I want to make you a promise though, so you'll make everything all right, and I can earn your love. I want to be humble—in a proud way. I want to know that my humility made you do something. But I guess that's not the kind of humility you look for.

So I'm stuck knowing I can't buy miracles or twist your mighty arm, and that I've never been your best friend, so I don't deserve any favors. And I wish I could live again and have faith. I wish I could learn to believe in words if only so that now I wouldn't be crying in the cold wishing wishing *wishing* for you to love me enough to save my sister's baby. And I wish there was a bargain I could make, but I know the child will die tonight.

And I want to be dead so it can live.

All my breath leaves me, alone on the sea floor, my tears adding infinitesimally, insignificantly to the indifferent swirls around me. My whole life exhaled. The useless body starts to rise, as if buoyancy, as if the air and light above beckoned it. And I am cold, and I am lonely, and I am leaving behind this world completely empty. I have failed.

...Then it rings.

Despite the cold, I spring up and grab the receiver. But I can't pick it up. It rings again, sharply, like a frightened baby needing held in the night. I don't want to hear this. Please, make it all right. Just care for us and love us enough to make everything all right. Please… God?

On the fourth ring I lift the receiver to my ear. "Hello," is all I can say.

Mom's crying, but it's a good cry. Sis is all right, and the baby, too. It'll have to stay in the hospital for awhile, though. And the police are looking for Dirk. (Please, use your billy clubs when you find him.) Mom says she wants to get home and get some sleep. She'll phone tomorrow.

I exhale a plume of anxiety. I can go in now.

Well, you've done it. You've made me feel absolutely worthless. I mean, I started as nothing, and then you gave me something I could never be worthy of. I hope you're laughing your can off.

As I stretch, I see there's frost on the ground, except where I lay. I'm going to turn off those blinkin' lights and box them back up. I don't want to see another Christmas light all year. I open my door and feel the lingering warmth embrace me, yet I have to stop. I'm crying again, but it's a good cry. I can't think of one redeeming aspect about me, yet the only omniscient Being in the universe reached down and decided…

…Thank you.

My Garden Which Never Grows

The sun is leaving me for the day. It may be the closest friend I have anymore, and it never speaks. I'm sitting on the redwood patio my husband built over two decades ago. It is due for a new finish, but that will wait for the summer. This place has been neglected in the past, when it served only as a summer home. But now that I have moved here, I will have the time to make repairs. Time, after all, is all I have.

I've always managed to neglect the present, which, at least lately, has led me to regret the past. Quite a complimentary pair of personality defects. Oh well.

I say that whenever I reach an impasse of personal realization and pride: Oh well. It keeps me from admitting I'm wrong even when my errors are clear, which in turn keeps me from having to take responsibility. It's quick and evasive and can sound pleasant even when I'm not. A wonderful phrase.

I retired from my professorship after the spring semester. I taught western religion at a mid-sized university. To teach religion: what a thought! But this is what I thought I did for years. We would look through the Bible, read Augustine's writings, and Aquinas's, and those of a dozen theologians. But I doubt I ever taught religion. I taught words. I taught a history and a rhetoric and a culture.

I never saved a soul. I never taught religion.

This shouldn't be surprising, since I didn't have one myself. I was raised in a churchgoing family, a good family, and my parents were religious. But it wasn't something they could teach me any more than I could teach my students. Besides, my students weren't seeking salvation: they were seeking knowledge. Just as I was.

In the spring, I plant my flowers, which is how I've spent the day. My once-white gloves are dark with the earth and rest on the wood by my chair. The view from here was once magnificent. Only a hundred yards to the north, the field ended and the pool of forest began to trickle up the mountain. But now only treetops are visible above the neighbors' privacy fences, and the mountain is occluded by split-level homes with windows larger than those in churches.

My home is perched on one of the few naturally level spots on this entire mountain. We chose the lot together, my husband and I. A rare event: us doing something together. Or maybe I should say having a unified purpose was uncommon. After all, we did things "together" all the time. Hard not to when you're married.

Funny. For all my claims of being a self-made woman, all of my accomplishments have involved family.

We drove out here one summer, about thirty-five years ago, to spend some time at the lake up north. We stopped in the town beneath the mountain for gas, but then stayed for a picnic lunch, and soon decided to spend the night. The morning found my husband and me hiking up this slope, stopping right on this small field. We looked over where we had come, looked how high there was yet to climb, and just enjoyed the view and air and trees, and each other. I didn't mean to suggest before that we were never in love. We were. We were until his death last spring, I think. But we had just forgotten to remind ourselves of it. We took for granted that all those years of marriage were a strong enough foundation for anything, and just quit building.

We lay and laughed on the field on the mountain until mid-afternoon, until we had to turn back before night caught us. David looked over the valley again, and I thought for a moment that was what love looked like: his eyes looking from the mountain with a something that could have been tears immune to gravity hovering in them. More than a longing. A *belonging*, but with a knowledge of parting.

"I wish we could live here," I said.

It was an approval for him to pursue the thought. We had commented all day how wonderful a place it was, though neither of us had imagined we would ever return. But when I saw his face, I thought we could capture forever that moment, and I wanted nothing more.

There were the most elegant flowers on the edge of the field in a corner created where two boulders met. Sometimes I remember the color as yellow, but wonder if they weren't really pink. Just a cluster of two: a cross between lilies and some hearty wildflower, maybe. I picked them and carried them down the mountain with me. With all the excitement of thinking of buying the field on the mountain I forgot about putting the flowers in water until we were packed and on the road. It was too late by then, I decided, and didn't bother asking David to pull over at a station. I'll see plenty of them when we build our home on the field, I thought. They withered in the back window while we drove on.

I don't know for sure what they were or where they came from: only that they were of the simplest beauty, and that I've never seen one since.

For years, I've been trying to grow a garden, but at this elevation, the cold kills all my efforts. Every time I get something planted, a cold snap comes. I was never much of a gardener, anyway, and haven't made too many beautiful things in my time, but, still, I wonder if Someone isn't having a little fun at my expense.

Maybe that's all life is: a cosmically grand and wry comedy. A slapstick with so many of us catching pies in the face, but only One throwing them from a distance.

I prefer not to think of it that way, though.

The one creation of beauty to my credit was not formed alone. It was a daughter. Mine, his. Even with this, though, a pie in the face. We created, and then we tore asunder. Love me. Become like me. Worship me and me alone. Pretend you are the creation I fool myself into believing I made. Pretend you truly came from me and not Someone else, and emulate me, not Him. But if parents are deities, then families are polytheistic, and children see the subtle war of the gods every night after school.

We destroyed her.

There's no use in crying over spilled milk. My mother used to say that often, which implies she had ample occasion to do so.

Looking back, I suppose she did. But maybe life isn't defined by what happens in it so much as by how you deal with it. There had to have been as many accidents, mistakes, and tragedies in my mother's life as in anyone else's, but she stayed kind and optimistic through it all. Maybe people aren't so much to be thought of as compendiums of events and dates and certificates of birth and death and all in between, but as characters: personalities.

That makes sense. I am not a college professor, anymore, but just a…just what I have been all my life, regardless of jobs or houses or paychecks. My daughter, too, is a personality. She can hardly be anything more to me. I don't know her last name, only that she married years back. I don't know her profession, or even if she has one. I know nothing of grandchildren, and probably never will, and probably don't deserve to. I'd only proselytize them to me. I'd only destroy the beauty which came from the beauty I destroyed long before. I would only obliterate the chance of expiation in this new generation.

My daughter took the best of both worlds. From my mother, sweetness to others; from me, a bitterness—which she returned.

The sweetness could also have come from David. It was wrong of me to include him in the blame. He didn't destroy her. I did. The constant coercion to please me is what ruined her. David loved her as she was for who she was: not a list of accomplishments, but a daughter. He was a good father, but we didn't work well as parents. He never said it to me, never told me to let her be herself, but that's the lesson she learned from him. If he had let me raise her my way, I wonder who my daughter would be now. I wonder if the situation would be the same.

Probably. I would still have driven her away—either by seeing what I am like and detesting this, as she has, or by becoming it herself. Neither could do anything but smother love. So it is not my daughter who harbors the hate. I have enough to give away, and the intended send it back.

The mountain is dark, except for a faint last wink from the sun as it sets in the valley. I pick up my gloves, and rise to go inside. I am cold as my last friend leaves me. Good night, dear Sun. Come back tomorrow.

Please.

The wind barrels down the mountain like an avalanche. It raids these houses and roads like a bandit, rummaging through our yards, scattering the order we have raked our lives into. It summons us to our doors and windows to see if someone is tapping on the glass—but it is only a swirling void waving the arms of trees against the houses. If you step outside, it washes about you, tangling your hair, breathing on your skin, and somehow reaching inside you—like Nostalgia—and holding your breath won't stop it. It stirs debris behind your clenched closed eyes and rigid frame. Violates recesses not forgotten but stored away like a trunk in the attic—things you can not discard, but which you don't care to view. Like seasons, settled, until the wind blows.

Shivering only tickles its malicious purpose.

On those days, the wind is my enemy. It causes torment outside my house, breaking branches, tipping flower pots, rattling fence gates—like a pack of jackals. But its most devious trick is keeping me inside the house and inside myself. Taunting, haunting, reminding, reaffirming the void so deep, so unforgettably recent.

I loved you, David, even if I neglected saying or showing it for so many years. It was never gone. It was only misplaced.

I never treated him right. Lord knows how it started, but it never ended. He resented my professorship. Not the position, but the requirements. It took my time and left so little for him. I didn't treat him like a woman should, I know, though he never said it. Except once.

He just wanted some time from me. Just some love.

"I don't see why we can't spend a few weeks at the mountain house," he said.

"I've told you, David, I'm writing an article. I can't write up there."

"Can't write up there? What better place could there be for it? No distractions, no… "

"No distractions? Of course. That's right, Dear, no distractions. No roads or television. Just fishing and hiking and the scenery. No sir, no distractions. Why, I'm sure I'll be able to get this article done, and maybe two more while we're there. When you aren't constantly begging affection and wanting all my time, that is."

He almost gave up right then. He never pursued a fight, except that once.

"That's right. I am always begging your affection. I do want to hold you and be with you and pretend every now and then that we're more than two people who share a house. I want you to be my wife. But I have to beg for it, and that's not how it should be. That is not how it should be."

I looked at him with my most faux-sympathetic eyes and said, "Oh well."

My “oh well” is something of the dark twin of my mother’s “no use crying.” Hers meant things will be all right despite the little accidents in life, so don’t let them bother you. Mine means things are not going to change despite the little problems in life, so get over them.

And David did, or tried to. I was always too busy reading papers or articles or going to conferences. But being a woman in the academy was not easy, and that’s what it took to get to the top of my field. Lot of good it did me. Where is my fame and power? Where are the colleagues I so impressed? They’ve gone on without me, ever pursuing their elusive knowledge. And where is my family? My husband is dead, and probably happier in the grave than he was for years with me. My daughter? My daughter is in the valley, and I am on my mountain.

On clear nights, I can sit on the patio and see the glow from the city a hundred miles away. The city where she lives—as far as I know. She could be gone, could be anywhere in the world, could be dead. But she was there last I knew, and that is where she is for me, now. Memory locates, and doesn’t amend until replaced by new memories. The glow is her glow, the city hers, and the distance between belongs to us both… but was a gift from me.

She used to call David, I know. He told me, but never repeated what she’d said. She asked him not to. That used to make me angry—that he wouldn’t tell his own wife about her own daughter—but if love is loyalty, then the two of them were bound to each other more strongly than to me, and rightly so.

I didn’t go to David’s funeral. I wanted her to be able to go and not have to deal with me. The occasion was sad enough.

Not surprisingly, either, I didn't care to be around people right then. David's passing was something I had to go through alone. Like everything else.

I've sat for hours and imagined her life. I've seen her husband as I picture him and the children they might have in the house they may live in. I've seen her laugh with her family. I've seen her open presents on Christmas. I've seen the children take their first steps, the dinner at Easter, the sprinkler showering the freshly mowed lawn. I have seen her life as best I can from this place, and I am happy for her. I only wish.... If I had...I'm so sorry, Baby. If I could wish on a star, it would land in your yard and your father would be there, and I would be there, and we could just try again. We could just try again to love each other all the same and I promise I won't ruin it this time with wanting more love than anyone else, because I know now that no one deserves any more love than anyone else, and if someone did, it wouldn't be me. I know now how to love you. I know after being with myself and no one else for so long that I could love you for being you, and not measure you against me, or anything else.

I know what it is to be alone, Baby.

No use crying over spilled milk.

My friend, my sun, smiles over me now. Hello, dearest. You will never know what a long thing a night is.

Another day in the dirt. More hopes of something blooming because of my effort. But if the rain floods these seeds, or the cold kills them, I will plant again and again until flowers grow here. I will not leave this world until I make something beautiful again. But what a woman must do is the greatest a woman can do: raise a beautiful child. How, I ask myself, can I do that now?

David never left me, never even threatened to. I don't really understand why, which, I think, points to the fact that it was love that kept him with me. I've never understood love. It has this quality of persistence. David tried and tried to make things better, and when I wouldn't let him succeed, he was there, anyway. He learned to live in the world I occupied, because he wanted to be with me.

But why? Lord, I was so cruel to him.

Like I said before, though, we were in love. That's another part of love I don't get: why he would spend so long waiting for me to show I loved him again. Maybe—and I only wonder at this—but just maybe love and memory live in the same place. Maybe love told memory not to give up, and memory told love not to let go.

If I love my daughter, then a persistence will see me through. Not a goal for myself like the love I had for my work, but a goal for her. That's what makes love so adamant: it won't let you give up when you want something for someone else. If it were only for yourself, you could surrender. But when it's for someone else, you can never give up, because you can't be sure *they've* had enough.

I won't say I understand love, but I think I know enough about it to let it help me find her.

After decades of diligent study, I've learned only a handful of things which can serve me any purpose now—and I may never even have the chance to use them—but I keep them secure in my memory, which I am beginning to think must be somewhere in the heart, and not the mind, and visit them every day so I will know them when I need them. One of these treasures is what my mother always said about there being no use crying over spilled milk. I know my mother didn't make that up, but she learned for herself what it meant for her. And, though, due to the many times I heard her say it, I could never have forgotten the phrase, I still had to find what it meant to me. And I have. I can look back and reminisce and regret and wish to God I wasn't the person I was to my loved ones, but that is all past. I can not change it. And the present? It seems I have always been determined to convert it into a past I could lament.

What milk is spilling now? What quiet, precious essence is flowing ever further from me?

My daughter? She is gone. Oh well. But there I betray myself. I could try to give up now before taking the responsibility, but I know this need to find her is not for me. I can say I don't know where she is or how to find her, or even who she is, now, so how can I even start to look for her? I can say that she never could love me and I never could be worthy of her love, anyway, so why try finding her, why try building some way over or around this pain? I could martyr myself in my own self-pity by proving I've been immune to love all along. Or I could find her.

But how?

I have found my own truism. I have unearthed my own treasure from the desert sands of my life. It is another of those few things I have learned. Want to know what knowledge I finally found, though perhaps too late? Listen: You can't win a race of the heart with your mind. Simple enough? Then why do I see so much of me in so many people? Why do I want to tell them all and make them understand? Why will they have to learn for themselves?

This may sound strange coming from a teacher and writer of informative articles, but I don't think we learn as readily as we think we do. We memorize easily enough. We read words from texts and know what they say, but to know what they *mean*, we must first come to the same conclusion ourselves through our own experiences. Then the words engraved in our memories are engraved in our lives as well. The words we finally find, and think "If only I had seen them sooner I wouldn't have had to have gone through that," are vivid paintings of our own mistakes. But there's no other way. Who can tell you the flavor of chocolate until you've tasted it yourself? Reading words written by others won't actually take you anywhere: at best, they're a map of where you, too, might go. We must discover for ourselves—which isn't so bad. Experience is what makes us human. Otherwise, we would be encyclopedias.

Morning again, and again I am in my garden which never grows. I have been considering something: Maybe the work of beauty I need to effect is not a creation at all, but another destruction. What good is there in creating love when hate stands in the way? Can they both be in the same place? I don't know, but I think there must be an eradication of the hate I have so casually distributed to her. And maybe that's what love is, more than something which brings two people together: something which keeps all else out.

I must span the chasm I've created. I must give my daughter the love she deserves, and must destroy the hate. But how?

Whatever happened to those beautiful flowers which grew here? Some things just happen naturally and can't be re-created no matter what amount of effort you put into it. Some things we take for granted, I suppose, and abuse. Again, there's nothing new to that thought, but it took me a lifetime to learn what it meant to me.

Night. No sun. Alone. No David, except in my heart: Memory. Nothing in my heart, except memory. And a little love. Just enough for me—something I've searched for without myself while it lay within. Just enough for her.

Funny. Love and hate seem to act the same way. When you give hate, you receive it again. When you give love, the same. No matter which you give, it takes only a little to receive an abundance in return.

Alone in bed with my thoughts, which revolve about the same thing: how to find my daughter.... If this is a thing of love, then it is of the heart. If it is of the heart, then the mind has no place in this search. The heart tells me to find her. Where? Where memory last knew her. In the city. Call the last number you had for her, the heart says. Work from there, it says, all I have is a memory. No deduction. No logic. Just a memory. *Follow me*, the heart says, *and you will find your daughter.*

The heart and its memory urge me to leave my bed, and I do. I follow them to the den and turn the desk lamp on. I know where it is. My heart knows. It's written on an envelope which I had ready when I called information to find her a year ago—when her father died. But her aunt called me that same day and told me she'd asked for me not to contact her. She could get all the information through her aunt, so I had no excuse to call her. But I put the envelope in the desk, thinking someday I'd have something to say to her. I finally do.

I sit in the chair on the deck, in the fading blue-black of night departing, with a blanket around me and an envelope in my hands. Come friend, dear sun, and see the smile on my face. It is a timid smile, painted with hope, but brushed by uncertainty. Still, it is a smile, and I want to share it with a friend. And there is more, dear sun. There is someone I hope to have you meet, if she will let me. There is a chance I will take today. And if I have no luck, I will try again and again, and I will not leave this world until I have done something of beauty. I have asked my heart to give me strength to do this, but it said it has no strength: it has only humility. And that is how this must be done.

Good morning, friend. You are finally waking. And so am I.

This Great Divide

So you have a little Christmas wish and you walk out to the back end of the rail fence with the crisp but snowless ground crackling under your boots. You've come here countless times, and though it's your "secret place," your private place to sort through your thoughts, anyone who knows you knows where to find you and when it's all right to approach—maybe by the way you prop your right foot solidly on the bottom rail, and lean against your forearms on the top rail. It's well behind the house, but just shy of being occluded by the edge of the barn. You never really had to hide from anyone, anyway—except maybe when you experimented with smoking when you were nine—and you figured out that it's easier to be left alone when you're in the open than when you seek shelter. If you try to be alone, that's when everyone suddenly thinks you need them around. This is where you stood on summer days as the crop duster swooped overhead, having raced toward you dangerously low and fast, wobbling and rocking from one wing-tip to the other, somehow graceful in its perilous way. Then, right at the fence where you stood, often with your friends, bicycles discarded on the sparsely weeded rough dirt behind, the unsteady plane would cut its spray and swan dive toward the clouds. Even if you didn't exactly shower in it, the cloud did mist over you in the wash of the wings. You didn't know a thing about cancer back then, and you don't pay it much concern now, figuring what's done is done, anyway, and there's bigger thoughts to take up your time.

After years of practice, you can recognize any make of car solely by the shape of its headlights at night, except for a few of the newer imports, since you haven't had much of a chance to inspect too many of them, and they all seem the same. But you can pick a Ford from a Chevy or a Jeep as soon as it comes over the rise almost a mile off. You can give the model year, most of the time, because of the amber lights bordering the headlights. Still, it's not a skill you bother trying to impress people with. It's just something you picked up while waiting for your father to come home. His will be the one with the driver's side light much brighter than the passenger side one, which you figure is due to burn out any time now, so you watch the "pop-eye" trucks coming at you, too. With the sun practically gone and the red glow washed along that western ridge, many of the cars still don't have their lights on. But you don't expect to see him this early, anyway.

You're not a rancher or a farmer, though you're pretty much surrounded by the both of them out here. The fence is your family's, and so is the land, but the crop belongs to a man who drives here earlier than you've ever woken on purpose, every morning for months. He has his own land, and rents a few acres here and there all the way between Cliffside and the junction. You don't see him this time of year except maybe at the store, but more often you see his wife. Still, you see more of him than of your father, and you don't want to be helpless like that little child you remember out here at this slowly rotting fence, but if there's a single wish you could have, you'd leave the gold and the dead in the ground and just have more time with him before it's too late.

Behind you, from the kitchen window, smatterings of sound are spilled into the lingering twilight as someone washes dishes at the sink, and someone else calls from deeper in the house with a request. Your aunt and her family arrived late this morning, always a few days early in these years since Mom left. It's all the family you have in the world, and for a moment the world seems like a very expansive place with no family in it. By now her eyes—because of course it's your aunt at the sink —have found you. She's probably been pausing at each window around the house, pulling the sheers aside inconspicuously for a cursory glance outside, making the maternal rounds, if you will. And maybe she stopped in the kitchen when she caught sight of you, and the dishes just seemed like a worthwhile way to occupy the time as she waited to see if you are all right. It must be hard being suspended between being a mother and being a stranger.

You can almost feel the warmth from the small window, where, if you turn, you will almost certainly see her figure. She's wiped the fog from the pane with a dry towel and her eyes are fixed on you, you imagine unpretentiously. And you expect that she's not concerned you might know. In fact, she'd probably welcome your coming to her and confiding everything. Or maybe not. You can't know for sure, so you don't risk burdening her. Besides, you're not sure you want to. You're well aware that your problems are probably just that: your problems. They're probably inflated to immensely awful proportions in your mind, you figure, and when you're so close to being considered something of an adult it sure wouldn't do any good to go whining about such trivial worries.

You'd like to just stay out there longer, but realize it won't do anything more than fuel her anxiety. The chill is starting to work its way beyond your skin, through your body. Those headlights won't be coming, you know. Not until after dark. But even if you're almost an adult, maybe there's no harm in wishful thinking, as long as no one else knows. So, before someone feels obligated to fetch you, you voluntarily stroll back to the house, careful to wear a light smile as you enter so no one thinks you're being moody. No need to drag down the rest of them.

"Oh! Hi there!" she chirps in surprise as you go in the kitchen door. It's hard to tell if the surprise is real, or if she's just acting like she wasn't watching you. "I thought you were in the living room with the boys."

"Nah," you say. "I was just taking care of a few things outside."

"Well, Don and the boys are in watching TV, if you want to join them."

She doesn't even realize she speaks as if it's her house. Doesn't matter, though. She is the mother, here.

Your Uncle Don is in your father's second-hand recliner, the one you practically had to twist his arm to buy at the garage sale after your mother took off with all your furniture. Again, you know it doesn't matter, but it's a territorial thing. This is where your father sits when he gets home. He takes off his cumbersome work boots and just relaxes for a few minutes as you heat up dinner. Sometimes, often, he falls asleep during the news. You've learned not to wake him before it gets late, because if you do he insists he's not tired, and that it's too early to go to bed, anyway.

You sit on the floor near the couch, where your two cousins share a comic book.

"Boys," your uncle says. "Scoot over. Make room for your cousin up there."

“Nah, it’s all right,” you say, though they’re already obediently huddling toward one end of the couch.

“Don’t be silly,” he says. “We don’t want to make you sit on the floor in your own house.”

You get up on the couch mostly because he’s made such a production out of it, and you are genuinely appreciative for the effort, though you often sit on the floor, anyway.

“What do you want to watch tonight?” Uncle Don asks, extending part of the newspaper toward you. The arm of the vinyl couch moans as you lean across it to accept the paper, but you realize looking at the weekly TV programming guide from the Sunday paper that your life is merely a compilation of second rate made-for-TV holiday specials, so you break into a grin that you decide not to try to explain to your uncle, who is trying to seem disinterested, though you are aware he’s practically studying you. He’s not a bad guy, but you’ve never been able to talk to him about something you are interested in. It’s always his topics, his memories. Anyone can learn to appease him by listening with an attentive appearance, but it takes a lot out of you, and you’re not up to it tonight.

“I don’t much care,” you say. “Whatever you want.”

Your father has dreams. He has dreams of you going to the university and becoming whatever you want. “Whatever it takes,” he sometimes says enthusiastically. But you watch him working himself to death to give you a better life and if you had just one wish, this wouldn’t be it. You’ve tried to get a job in town, but everything from the supermarket to the hardware store to the gas station is always fully staffed, with waiting lists longer than your family’s history in these parts. Everybody’s hurting some, and they take care of their own first. You can't really hold that against them, but you wish there were more of "your own" here, too. And you wonder if part of what drives your father is that he wants to give you everything. You think maybe he still wants your mom to come back, and maybe that he thinks if he could have given her more that she would have stayed. But you don't want more things: you want more of him. Still, you're afraid. Afraid that maybe this drive to please you is all he's got left in his fuel tank, and if you take that away from him, too, he might just wear down altogether.

"You're a senior this year, right?" your uncle asks during the commercials.

"Yeah."

"Thought about where you're going to college?"

"Well, you know how it is these days. I guess I might go up the road to the community college for a year or two."

"Got any idea what you want to major in?" he asks.

"Wildlife management, maybe. We'll see."

"Any jobs in that? Wildlife management? What would you be, a park ranger?"

"Would you fight forest fires?" your younger cousin, Danny, asks.

"Nah, I wouldn't be fightin' fires. I'd be keeping track of the animals, mostly, I suppose. I'm not exactly sure."

"You wanna work in Yellowstone, or something?" Uncle Don asks.

"Yeah, or maybe Glacier," you say, cutting yourself short, because the program is back on, and your uncle's head has turned toward the television.

Next to the sofa that used to rest along the wall beneath the window, there was an end table which had a door, like a cabinet. Inside there was a picture album. The first page was of your parents' wedding. You never recognized many of the people, anyway, but it looked like a pretty happy time. A few pages later, there were some shots of your mother still young, with a glowing face, posing for a profile shot. She was pregnant with you. Then you were born, and captured on film, too. From that point on, most of the pictures were of you, or you and your father, or you and your mother, but hardly ever everyone in the same frame. You'd flip through that album on occasional rainy Sunday afternoons when you were young, and your mother would narrate. Even though there's nothing that you absolutely long for or miss, it would be nice to browse through that album right now.

Soon there would come pages of this house when your family bought it. You remember that. It was exciting. The mill was booming, so lots of folks were buying up land outside of town. It was like living in the suburbs. Now it's life in the boonies. Your mother had a lot to do with getting the place, you remember. It was her initiative, her idea, her dream. You were all of six, but these are things that stay polished in your memory. The houses were spaced out, as everyone wanted their land, so nights were always quiet, except for the invariable rig passing by on the highway. Cars only made sleek sounds like skimming the surface of still water; but sometimes the rigs would use their brakes suddenly, and make that noise like the whole thing was crashing in on itself. "Another antelope on the road," your dad might say.

By bus, it took nearly forty minutes to get home from school, because they had to let off the kids who lived closest first. No one your age lived anywhere near you, though, so your mother sometimes let you go home with a friend after school to play. She would come get you in time to make dinner before your father got home. Or sometimes a friend would come home with you. Seven miles from town. Times were pretty good.

The mill stands about five miles on the other side of town. It had its boom during the first years of your elementary school education. But by middle school, they were talking lay-offs. And when you were in the eighth grade your father no longer came home for dinner. There had been a strike, a walk-out, lay-offs. You name it. When the dust settled, about forty percent of the workers were still employed, and they were quite obligated to work twelve hour days, and felt grateful for the opportunity to do it, too. Your father was one of the lucky few.

More and more, the twelve mile drive to the mill became just more thankless overtime. And life here became quieter, lonelier than Pluto's moon. Your mother was detached already. So you really weren't as shocked as you should have been when she packed up and left.

"Boys! Get washed up for dinner!" your aunt calls from the kitchen doorway.

"All right!" they answer, instantly, though not hurriedly, moving for the bathroom.

"Aren't we waiting on Dad?" you ask, instinctively, before you realize it might sound snappy.

"Of course," she says. "He gave me strict instructions to have dinner on the table at eight, sharp, though. And I do need to feed the boys before they starve to death, Honey."

"This boy, too!" your uncle calls over the back of the recliner.

You go to the front window to check the highway, but you can't see much of it from that side of the house. "I'll be out front!" you call to your aunt.

"Well, dinner's just about ready," she says.

"I know. I'll just be right outside."

"All right. I'll call you."

You shut the warmth and talk and television inside and passively wish you had worn a jacket. Nights are deceptively chilly. Keeping an eye on the road, you fetch an armful of firewood at a time and fill up the rack near the kitchen door. Then you switch on the barn light and splinter off some kindling on the old stump. No sign of him yet.

What are your dreams? More than dreams you have fears. You fear being stranded with no job, no way to keep going, but having to keep going all the same. A while back, you had a dream which was almost like a fantastically vivid painting because you can't really remember any movement—though there must have been—but just the sensations of being caught on that canvas. You stood beside your father, who stood beside his car, which rested alongside the highway which runs along your field. Only it wasn't your field. It had unimaginable flowers, like that giant meadow of poppies in *The Wizard of Oz*. It was your highway, though. You remember the network of tar lines, like a magnified alligator's back, running across and along every few feet for the miles of straight miles that the highway extended. In that direction your mother walked. It seemed they had fought—she had fought, he had complacently responded—that it was time to be going, but he wanted to look some more at all those flowers and the mountains beyond them and the sun and sky beyond those. You can't remember there being anything spoken, but you remember she meant, "You're wasting your life." And he meant, "This is my life."

You remember the magnetism of watching your mother leave you, and sensing that it was all right, after all. For here there was another attraction. She walked east, and east could always be held. But further, over that low but visually insurmountable rise, lay the west. The west was where you would go. But now you would wait with your father. It was, after all, as beautiful as Heaven.

Yet the dream was only a trite community theater production of the truth. It hadn't really been like that. Your father's mother was going under for surgery, and he was heading home to be with her, since the rest of the family couldn't make it. Your mother said that they couldn't afford for them both to go, and she hoped he'd be fine going alone. He should have known something was wrong when she talked about money as if it were finite.

He drove out of sight down the east stretch of the highway. You waved from the fence. The next day, your mother was up early, and somehow had a moving van which two stocky men were loading with what you had thought was your furniture. She didn't answer when you asked her, "What's going on, Mom?"

She kept herself busy, packing and even helping the men load, but it only took less than two hours, and as the furnishings and boxes spilled out of your home and into the back of that truck like the sand from an hourglass, you realized that there was no more reason on this earth to treat your mother like a mother, and you grabbed her by the arm as she once again tried to slip by you.

"Tell me what's going on!" you shouted at her.

"We're… listen," she said. "Listen… we need to… just let me put this box in the truck, and we'll talk."

You looked at her and realized that your anger had already peaked, and that frustration was losing the bout to desperation and anxiety, so you let her go and followed her to the doorway, watching as she gingerly set the box inside the truck, then came back inside. She sat on a kitchen chair, you leaned against the counter. The room held only the two of you, two chairs, and a few wads of newspaper leftover from wrapping the dishes you had naively planned to continue eating off of.

"Well, kiddo," she said, "I guess you can see…" Then she started to break down. "You can see… I'm going."

"Why? Where are you going?" you asked, leading her like a child.

" I'm… Oh, honey, you just don't understand! I can't… What's going on is just… Oh, honey!" Then she really started to cry. "Just, you know I love you. You know that. So, just tell your father I'm so sorry."

You watched her cry for a moment, but maybe knew in that one morning you had already stopped loving her. You looked at her like she was an actress, and she wasn't about to convince you of how much she was hurting when you were the one who would still be standing there when everyone else pulled away, and you were the one who would have to be brave enough to break your own father's heart.

You watched her go, without being offered a hug. That evening… well, that evening was hard for you. Except for your room, which she had left alone, and your father's things, which were now stacked in neat little piles on the floor of his so vacant bedroom, you didn't have but an end table and a roll of toilet paper in the whole damned house. In the sun's hazy golden wake, you set up a few old cans on the fence and knocked 'em down again with a pellet gun from thirty yards. But that was just to keep you from thinking. You realized that, if you ever started, you had already stopped hating your mother, even resenting her. But you couldn't say that you loved her again. That truly had all come to an end that morning. Still, you had wanted her to come home, just so that you wouldn't have to see the look on your father's face.

After four days of waiting for your mother to come home, of hoping she'd at least call, but mostly hoping she'd come home before Dad knew she was gone, and before she was gone so long it meant she was gone for good, a little bird told you she wasn't coming home. You hated that bird enough to finally cry. The next day, your father pulled up the drive.

Your mother called a few days after he arrived. He had been in a minor state of shock, though not panic, until then. After that single phone call, he seemed all right. Really. He got the answers he needed, apparently. The most shocking thing about your mother's departure was that your father remained strong, focused. But he had to be. Mom had taken everything solid from you, and your father had to start over the very next day by buying anything to start filling the house up again. You ate canned food off of paper plates for about ten days. Meanwhile, you learned to cook, fast, and learned how to shop, too.

The UPS truck delivered new dishes another week later, and periodically brought other items ordered from the JC Penney or Sears catalogs. But your father needed to be frugal. See, your mother had racked up some sizable numbers on their credit cards. Even the things she took from under you weren't paid for. So your father worked diligently to pay off things he didn't even own, and tried to put together some sort of life for himself with the leftovers. "I guess she deserved something after so many years," he said once, as if he were admitting life had been punishment for her. But you were alive and aware all that time, and you knew full well that only the end had been hard. You knew how well he treated her, and you started to resent her again because she was breaking a man who was carrying all the world that you could see on his back.

Not long after she left, mandatory overtime was lifted and a voluntary system began. Your father, burdened as he was, kept working the long shifts. He still does. He's got those old credit card bills just about whacked, and everything in this house is paid for. But the house is a burden all its own. No one could afford to buy it after the mill's troubles, and he certainly can't afford to buy a second home simultaneously, so he's stuck out here in the home his wife wanted. You're thinking of telling him, maybe even tonight, that you want to go into the military for a few years before college, even though he knows it isn't true. But you think you can convince him. You think that maybe the relief that he'll feel when he hears that will be enough to make him accept it. And, honestly, though you've never considered yourself a soldier, you figure it won't be all that bad, and that it's worth it to see him come home in the daylight again. No matter what happens, whether you spend a year or two at the community college nearby, or enlist, you'll be leaving soon, and you'll be more worried about him then. You need that time, that time you've been missing. You need it everyday for the rest of the days you have together, and you need it to start now. So you drop the kindling in the box by the firewood, and though you can hear your aunt calling you from the front door, you just respond, "O.K.," then wander off and assume your normal position at that fence, and consider maybe going in to get a jacket. But, no, he'll be coming home real soon.

About the Author

Eric Prochaska was born and raised in Iowa, except for a few years when he lived in California. Those years nourished a fondness for the American West, and solicited his return to the West when he moved to Arizona in 1990. Eric teaches English writing in Seoul, South Korea. He is currently working on a second collection of stories, as well as a novel.

A note to our readers

We invite you to share your thoughts and reactions to these stories online at www.haloforgepress.com. And, of course, we hope you will share these stories with those close to you.

At our website you can also find news about upcoming projects from Halo Forge Press and Eric Prochaska.

We thank you for reading this book and supporting independent presses and booksellers across America. Keep Small Town America strong—buy local!

If you would like to use this book in a book discussion club, or if you would like to buy copies for resale, please contact us via our website for discount information.

Thank you for your support.